CONTENTS

STORIES BY **IAN ROBINSON**
ILLUSTRATED BY **JOHN HARROLD**
STORY COLOURING BY **GINA HART**

© Express Newspapers 2000

John Harrold.

This book belongs to:

. . . .

RUPERT

John Harrold.

THE
EXPRESS
ANNUAL

Pedigree®

No 65

Published by Pedigree Books Limited
The Old Rectory, Matford Lane, Exeter, Devon, EX2 4PS

RUPERT and

*The chums run out of school with glee.
"Come on!" calls Rupert. "Follow me!"*

Rupert and his chums have just finished school for the day. "I really enjoyed today's art class!" Ottoline tells Dr. Chimp. "Good!" smiles the teacher. "Next time we'll all work together on a big picture of Nutwood..." As Rupert and Bill stroll across the common, they see a group of pals gathered round a poster on a tree. "I wonder what it's for?" asks Bill. "Everyone looks very excited..." "Perhaps it's the Circus?" suggests Rupert.

the Fool's Prize

The others are all gathered round
A bright new poster they have found...

"A Fool's Day Festival!" Bill cries.
"Look, Rupert! There's a Best Jest prize!"

Rupert and Bill are surprised to find that the poster is for a Fool's Day Festival... "Best Jest Competition!" reads Rupert. "Prizes for the best pranks and riddles..." "Join in on April Fool's Day!" calls a voice. "Fun for everyone. Laughter for all!" As the chums look up, a flurry of brightly-coloured paper falls from the sky like a shower of confetti. "A hot-air balloon!" cries Rupert. "I wonder whose it can be?"

Then, suddenly, they hear a call
And sheets of paper start to fall...

RUPERT SEES THE JESTER

"The Jester, with a megaphone!"
cries Rupert. "Why, I might have known!"

"He wants us all to try and play
A joke to celebrate Fool's Day..."

"A Fool's Day Prize!" laughs Mr. Bear.
"We'll all join in, so just beware!"

That night, as Rupert lies in bed,
Jokes, pranks and riddles fill his head...

As the balloon drifts over Nutwood, Rupert catches sight of the pilot and gives a cry of recognition. "The Jester! Of course, I should have guessed..." The others remember the Jester too, and how he spends the whole year writing jokes and riddles for Christmas crackers. "Fun on the First!" he calls through a megaphone. "Prizes for pranks and a party for all..." "That's what this leaflet says!" smiles Bill. "He's holding a special Fool's Day party and everyone in Nutwood is invited."

When Rupert arrives home he finds that his parents have heard about the Jester's party too. "This leaflet came through the letter-box!" laughs Mrs. Bear. "Fancy having a prize for the best jest!" says Rupert's father. "The first of April will be even riskier than normal if everyone in Nutwood tries to catch each other out." When Rupert goes to bed that night he lies awake, thinking of what to do. "Should it be a riddle or a trick?" he murmurs, then suddenly he has a good idea...

RUPERT VISITS BILL BADGER

"Come on, Bill! You and I can win
The Jester's Prize, so let's begin…"

"We'll need the stilts you had last year,"
"All right!" says Bill. "I keep them here…"

At first the chums fall off, but then
They get the hang of stilts again…

"Hello!" calls Algy, cheerfully.
"I've something here you ought to see…"

Next morning, Rupert sets out bright and early to visit his chum, Bill Badger. When he reaches Bill's house he tells him he has had a good idea for a prank they can play… "Wonderful!" says Bill. "I knew you'd come up with something!" Rupert points to the garden shed and asks Bill if he still has a pair of stilts. "Somewhere!" laughs his chum. "Do you remember how we learnt to use them last summer? At first it seemed impossible…" Opening the door, he gives a cry of triumph. "Look, there they are!"

Rupert and Bill take turns at walking on the stilts. "See how far you can go!" laughs Bill. "It's not as easy as it looks…" Rupert sets off across the garden, then peers precariously over the hedge. "I can see the whole road from up here!" he calls. "And I can see you!" laughs Algy. "Walking on stilts! For a moment there, I thought you must have grown!" Algy tells the chums that he has come to show them a special flower. "I'm wearing it in my button-hole," he smiles.

RUPERT AND ALGY ARE AMBUSHED

*"Look!" Algy laughs. "I'll show you how
My button-hole squirts water now..."*

*But then the Fox twins join in too
And leave the ambushed chums soaked through...*

*The Foxes run off, full of glee,
"We'll win the Fool's Prize easily!"*

*"Come on!" says Rupert. "You and I
Can beat them if we really try!"*

Rupert peers over the hedge at Algy's button-hole. "Very nice," he smiles. "But why is it so special?" "Watch!" laughs Algy as the flower sends out a sudden jet of water. "It's lucky for you you're out of range!" Just then, the pals are joined by Freddy and Ferdy Fox. "Take that!" they cry, squirting the pair with water pistols. "We're the best pranksters in Nutwood!" laughs Freddy. "Everyone else might as well give up. We're bound to win the Jester's prize!"

"I'm drenched!" splutters Algy as the Fox brothers run off, laughing. "Me too!" says Rupert. "The trouble with Freddy and Ferdy is they're always playing pranks. They never know when to stop..." As Algy goes home to change his clothes, Rupert and Bill carry on preparing their own Fool's Day plan. "We'll take the stilts round to my house now," says Rupert. "I'm sure we can beat the Foxes when it comes to clever pranks!" "I hope so!" nods Bill. "Those two would be unbearable if they won."

RUPERT AND BILL SET TO WORK

The two pals question Mrs. Bear.
Does she have any wood to spare?

Inside the shed they find a plank
That's just right for their Fool's Day prank...

"Trick footprints!" Bill laughs. "What a size!
They're bound to win the Jester's prize..."

"We'll wait until it's dark tonight.
Till then, let's keep these out of sight..."

As soon as the chums reach Rupert's house, they ask his mother if they can have some old wood from the garden shed. "Of course!" she says. "But do be careful if you're using any tools..." Inside the shed, Rupert sorts through a stack of timber until he finds a piece of board. "Just what we need!" he smiles. "There's enough here for two." "One for each stilt!" nods Bill. "Draw them out and we'll make a start. I can hardly wait to see how they'll work."

Taking a pencil from his father's tool-box, Rupert draws two identical shapes on the piece of board... "Giant footprints!" laughs Bill. Soon the pals have made a pair of huge wooden feet, which they fix to the bottom of their stilts. "Brilliant!" laughs Bill. "They'll fool the whole of Nutwood. All we have to do is wait until dark." "I hope it works!" says Rupert. "We can't risk practising yet, in case someone sees. Let's go in for tea now, then come back later..."

RUPERT'S TRICK BEGINS

As darkness falls, the chums set out.
"There isn't anyone about!"

They reach a small pond, "This looks fine!
It's time to try this plan of mine..."

On tall stilts, Rupert starts to stride
Across the pond to the far side.

He clambers out and soon the pair
Leave muddy footprints everywhere...

As soon as it is dark, Rupert and Bill take the stilts from the garden shed and hurry away to the edge of the common. "I'm glad there's nobody about!" says Bill. "With a bit of luck we won't be seen at all..." The pair keep going until they reach a small duckpond. "This should be fine!" smiles Rupert. "Not too deep but good and muddy at the bottom." "Good luck!" laughs Bill as Rupert takes the stilts. "I'll wait here with the torch while you set off..."

Clambering on to the stilts, Rupert strides slowly towards the pond then wades straight towards the middle, scattering the startled ducks as he goes. "Well done!" cheers Bill. "How does it feel?" "Muddy!" laughs Rupert. "I'll just walk round a few times then we can set out..." As soon as Rupert is ready, Bill switches on his torch and leads the way along a lane towards Nutwood. "It's working!" cries Rupert. "Our giant has just left his first set of footprints!"

RUPERT MAKES A STRANGE TRAIL

The footprint trail spreads into town
As Rupert wanders up and down...

Then Bill spots Growler. "Let's wait here,
I'll tell you when the coast is clear!"

"We'll end the giant's trail by this wall!"
Laughs Rupert. "That should fool them all..."

"I'll hide the stilts away. What fun!
Tomorrow we'll trick everyone!"

As Rupert follows Bill through the deserted streets of Nutwood, he leaves a trail of enormous, muddy footprints. "They really do look as though they were made by a giant!" laughs Bill. "I can't wait to see what everyone says when they find them tomorrow..." Stopping suddenly, he switches off the torch and gestures for Rupert to stop. "Growler!" he hisses. "He must be making his evening rounds!" "Wait till he's gone, then we'll finish off." says Rupert. "It shouldn't take much longer..."

As soon as P.C. Growler has gone on his way, the chums set out again, leaving a trail of muddy footprints behind them. "This is where the giant jumped over a wall, then vanished!" laughs Rupert. He stops abruptly and jumps down from the stilts. Giggling with mirth, the pals run back towards their houses, with Bill promising to hide the stilts before anyone sees. "See you tomorrow!" calls Rupert. "I bet our trail fools everyone! The whole village will be talking about it!"

Next morning, Rupert's keen to see
What sort of jokes and pranks there'll be.

The first is one that Mrs. Bear
Has planned to catch him unaware...

"Feathers! What a good trick to play!
We'll have to be on guard today..."

"What's this?" blinks Mr. Bear. "Oh, dear!
*Now **I've** been caught as well, I fear!"*

Next morning, Rupert hurries down to breakfast as soon as he wakes. "Hello!" smiles Mrs. Bear. "You're in a hurry!". "Bill and I thought we'd make an early start!" he laughs. "We don't want to miss any jokes...". "Come and have some cereal," says Rupert's mother. "I've already got you a bowl and spoon..." Rupert picks up the packet and starts to pour it out. "Feathers!" he cries in astonishment. "April Fool!" chuckles Mrs. Bear. "I caught you fair and square!"

"A bowl of feathers!" laughs Mr. Bear. "I wonder what they taste like?" Shaking his head, he sits down in his favourite chair and starts to read the paper. At first everything seems normal, but, as the paper unfolds, a row of cut-out figures appear, linking arms across the front page... "How? What? Good gracious!" blinks Rupert's father. "April Fool!" laughs Mrs. Bear. "That's two of you I've caught and the morning's hardly started. Perhaps *I'll* win a prize."

RUPERT'S PRANK FOOLS EVERYONE

The postman tells how he's just seen
Huge footprints where a giant has been...

A crowd all marvel at the sight
While Bill stands chuckling with delight.

"We've fooled them all!" the pals agree.
Then someone calls – "It's Gregory!"

He points to something odd he's found –
"A banknote, lying on the ground!"

Still smiling at his mother's joke, Rupert sets out to see what everyone else is up to... "Morning, Rupert!" calls the postman. "You'll never guess what I've just seen! Enormous footprints - all along the High Street. I've never known anything like it!" As Rupert hurries along the road he spots a crowd of people, peering at the footprints and shaking their heads in disbelief. His chum, Bill, is already there, watching newcomers marvel in surprise at the mysterious trail.

"Look at these footprints!" cries Bill. "They must have been left by a giant..." "I wonder?" laughs Rupert, winking at his chum. Just then, the pair hear Gregory Guineapig calling from the other side of the road. "Come and see what I've found!" he cries. As Rupert gets nearer he spots a five-pound note, lying on the grass. "Somebody must have dropped it!" he says. "You ought to give it to P.C. Growler." "I will if I can catch it!" says Gregory. "The wind keeps blowing it away..."

RUPERT MEETS THE JESTER AGAIN

*The chums are both amazed to see
The note move unexpectedly...*

*Then Podgy takes them by surprise –
"I really fooled you both!" he cries.*

*"Bravo!" the Jester calls. "Well done!
I'm glad to see you're having fun..."*

*He writes down Podgy's name. "Now tell
Me all the other pranks as well..."*

Gregory tries to pick up the banknote. "You see!" he tells Rupert. "As soon as I get near, it flutters away!" The chums try together, but with no more success... "How strange!" murmurs Rupert. "It doesn't even seem very windy!" Just then, he hears the sound of laughter as the banknote flies into the air. "April Fool!" cries Podgy, stepping out from behind the hedge. "I caught you both, didn't I?" "Yes," admits Gregory. "I'd no idea you were pulling it along. What a clever trick!"

"I agree!" calls a voice. "First rate fooling! Ten out of ten!" To the chums' amazement, the Jester suddenly appears over the top of the hedge with a notebook in his hand. "I like the giant footprints too!" he cries. "Fooled half the village! They all looked quite worried until I reminded them of the date." The Jester's spring-heeled shoes send him bouncing round the pals in huge leaps and bounds. "Any other riddles to report?" he asks. "Prizes for all, from playful pranks to jolly japes..."

RUPERT LEADS THE WAY

*The Jester tells the pals to find
A signpost he has left behind...*

*"I know the one he means! Let's see,
It's not far off, just follow me!"*

*They spot the sign and start to run
Towards it, "Come on, everyone!"*

*"This way!" reads Rupert. "Off we go!
We'll be the first ones at the show..."*

The Jester finishes making his list of jokes, then tells the chums he is off to look for more. "All's fair till twelve!" he laughs. "After that the joke rebounds..." As he speaks, he jumps higher and higher, then bounces over the hedge. "See you at the party!" he calls. "Follow the signs and you won't get lost." The chums are baffled until Rupert tells them about a signpost he knows that points to the Jester's house. "That's where the trail must start!" he smiles. "Come on! I'll show you the way..."

Rupert has already told his chums how he first met the Jester by following a trail across the common. "It started at a strange signpost which didn't seem to point anywhere," he explains. "When Willie and I found it, we still didn't know which way to go..." To Rupert's surprise, he finds that the sign has changed. "This way," he reads. "It looks quite straightforward! I suppose the Jester's decided to stop playing pranks for a day and leave the jokes to us for a change."

RUPERT CROSSES A BRIDGE

As Rupert leads the way, he sees
Another signpost near some trees...

The Fox brothers are searching too –
"Hello! We've found another clue!"

The Foxes tell the pals that they
Would rather Rupert leads the way...

"Come on!" he calls. "I'm sure it's fine.
We'll cross this bridge and read the sign!"

Heading off in the direction of the signpost, Rupert and his chums follow the path across the common until they find more signs, all pointing the way with large arrows... "This is easy!" laughs Rupert. "We'll soon be at the Jester's house." To his surprise, the Fox brothers are already standing by the next arrow, looking anxiously at the path ahead. "Hello, Rupert!" calls Ferdy. "I see you're on your way to the Jester's party. He told us all we had to do was follow the arrows."

When he looks at the path ahead, Rupert understands why the Foxes were puzzled. "The path seems to cross the river and continue on the far side!" says Freddy. "I thought we'd end up in Popton, but Ferdy's sure we should carry on..." Rupert peers into the distance. "There's another sign on the far bank!" he laughs. "The Jester must mean us to cross over, then follow the trail when we get to the other side." "Right you are!" nods Ferdy as Rupert crosses the river. "You lead the way and we'll follow..."

RUPERT AND HIS PALS ARE STRANDED

The pals all gasp at what they see...
"A Fool's Day prank!" gasps Gregory.

"You're stranded now!" the Foxes jeer.
"We'll win the Jester's prize this year!"

"Goodbye!" calls Freddy. "See you when
You've found a way across again..."

"I say!" blinks Ottoline. "We're stuck!
We'll miss the party! What bad luck!"

Rupert's pals follow him across the narrow bridge to the far side of the river, then hurry to the next sign in the Jester's trail. "April Fool!" gasps Ottoline. "What does it mean? I thought the Jester had given up pranks for the day?" "We haven't!" laughs Ferdy. "No!" chuckles Freddy as he pulls away the bridge. "I told you we'd outsmart you! Now we're bound to win the Jester's prize..." "Tricked!" groans Gregory. "We'll just have to wait here until they've finished gloating!"

"Stop!" calls Rupert as the Fox twins turn to go. "You can't just leave us stranded here..." "We can!" laughs Freddy. "That's the best part of the joke." "Come on!" calls Ferdy. "We don't want to miss the start of the party!" "What a pair!" says Ottoline. "It will take us ages to find another crossing." "They'll eat all the food!" gasps Podgy. "And claim the prize!" adds Gregory. "I wonder?" murmurs Rupert. "Things might not be as bad as they seem! I think I know a way to cross the river..."

RUPERT HAS AN IDEA

"Come on!" says Rupert. "I know how
We'll get across the river now..."

The pals all join in Rupert's plan
And find the biggest stones they can.

"An island! Now it's not too wide
For us to reach the other side..."

"Success!" calls Rupert, leaping clear.
"Well done!" the watching chums all cheer.

Rupert tells the chums that he doesn't think the river is nearly as hard to cross as it looks... "It's too wide to jump over, but it isn't very deep. If we can make a little island in the middle, we can hop over without getting wet at all!" The chums agree to try and set about finding some large stones to carry down to the water's edge. "This one first!" says Rupert. "We'll throw it right into the middle of the stream!" "Bravo!" cheers Bill as it lands with an enormous splash...

One after another, the chums throw their stones into the middle of the river. "It's worked!" laughs Gregory. "We've made a tiny island!" Rupert volunteers to be the first one across. "It's my idea, so I'll see if it works!" Taking a run up to the bank, he jumps on to the stone, then hops across to the other side with a whoop of triumph. "Well done!" cries Ottoline. "You didn't even get wet feet." "My turn next!" calls Bill. "If you can do it, so can I! Stand clear, everyone..."

*"The Foxes turned this arrow round
To stop the real path being found..."*

*"A sign!" cries Podgy. "Now we're back
To following the proper track!"*

*"The Jester's garden!" Rupert cries.
"This pathway's one I recognise!"*

*The Jester's strung balloons to show
His visitors the way to go...*

As soon as the last of the chums is safely across the river, they all hurry back along the path to the place where they met the Foxes. "I'll turn the sign back so it points the right way," says Rupert. "We don't want anyone else to take a wrong turn!" "I wonder how much further we'll have to go?" says Ottoline. "There's another sign!" calls Podgy. "At least we're on the right trail..." "Freddy and Ferdy will be surprised!" laughs Gregory. "They won't be expecting us for ages!"

As they hurry from sign to sign, the chums find the hedges by the side of the path growing higher and higher... "It's the beginning of the Maze!" says Rupert and explains how the Jester's house is right at the middle. The Jester's Maze is normally very hard to follow, with all sorts of tricky turnings and dead-ends. To the pals' surprise, they find the hedges are hung with bunches of brightly-coloured balloons. "Markers!" laughs Rupert. "It's just as well, or we'd never get through!"

RUPERT FINDS THE JESTER'S HOUSE

The Jester's house comes into view –
The Fox brothers have found it too...

"Hello!" smiles Freddy. "Glad you came!
Our little prank was just a game..."

When Podgy tries a plate of cakes
He's shocked to find that they're all fakes!

Rupert hears voices drawing near –
Then smiles as two more chums appear...

Following the trail, Rupert and his chums come to a garden, in the middle of which is the Jester's house. "Isn't it funny!" laughs Ottoline. "Everything's topsy-turvy..." "Hello!" calls Freddy Fox. "I knew you'd get here eventually. No hard feelings over our little prank?" "No!" laughs Rupert. "It is April Fool's Day, after all!" Looking around, he sees that the Foxes are the first to arrive. "Have you seen the Jester?" he asks. "No," says Freddy. "Only this table, with a plate of cakes..."

The chums decide to sit at the table with Freddy and Ferdy while they wait for the Jester to arrive... "I'm hungry after all that walking!" says Podgy. "I don't suppose anyone would mind if I tried a cake..." Everyone watches as Podgy takes a bite. "Urrgh!" he cries. "They're made of rubber!" "I fell for them too!" laughs Ferdy. "The Jester must have left them here to catch us unawares..." Just then the chums hear voices as Algy and Tigerlily arrive. "Hello!" laughs Algy. "We've made it."

RUPERT'S PALS ARE CAUGHT OUT

As Algy takes a look around
He stops to sniff a flower he's found...

He steps closer and bends to see –
The trick plant squirts him suddenly!

"How funny, Algy! What a sight!"
Laughs Tigerlily. "Serves you right!"

But then she finds more hidden jests
Are waiting for the party guests!

As Rupert tells the others all about the Jester's strange house, Algy Pug notices a big, yellow flower... "It's just like the one in my button-hole!" he laughs. "I wonder if it's very fragrant?" Leaning over to sniff the flower, Algy steps on to a ring of cobbles surrounding the Jester's flower-bed. All at once a jet of water shoots up from the centre of the flower, catching him full in the face... "Tricked!" he sputters. "Fancy falling for a prank like that!"

"I'm drenched!" grumbles Algy. "Serves you right!" laughs Tigerlily. "Going round Nutwood, squirting everyone with a trick flower!" "I know!" says Algy. "I never dreamt it would happen to me..." Tigerlily is laughing so much that she has to sit down on a nearby seat. "Help!" she gasps suddenly. To everybody's amazement the seat sinks to the ground, sending Tigerlily toppling off... "I don't believe it!" Rupert gasps. "The Jester's garden must be full of tricks and surprises!"

RUPERT LEARNS WHO HAS WON

*The Jester pops us from behind
A bush. "Last jokes! Hope you don't mind..."*

*"Your Fool's Day pranks have been such fun –
It's hard to pick a winning one!"*

*"The winners of the Fool's Day Prize
Are the Fox twins!" the Jester cries.*

*"Hurrah! We've won!" the Foxes cheer.
He goes to fetch their prize. "Wait here..."*

As the chums help Tigerlily to her feet they hear a rustle from the bushes and spot the April Fool himself... "Sorry about that!" he smiles. "I just couldn't resist a few little jokes of my own!" Welcoming the pals to the party, he tells them how much he has enjoyed all their Fool's Day tricks. "Giant footprints, joke banknotes, trick button-holes and all such fun! It hasn't been easy picking a winner, but at last I can reveal the name of Nutwood's prize prankster..."

Rupert and his chums can hardly wait to see who has won the Jester's trophy. "Freddy and Ferdy!" he announces. "A pair of prize pranksters who fooled you all!" "Oh, no!" groans Gregory. "Not the Fox twins! An award will make them even worse than before..." The rascally pair can hardly believe their luck as the Jester goes indoors to get their prize. "He must have seen our false trail!" chuckles Freddy. "It was rather good, wasn't it?" says Ferdy. "I wonder what we've won?"

RUPERT SEES THE FOXES' REWARD

The Jester brings the Foxes' treat.
Two creamy custard pies to eat...

"Congratulations! Now I'll serve
You with the prize your tricks deserve!"

"Your joke was too late, I'm afraid.
The rule demands you be repaid!"

"And now, it's time to start our tea
I'll count to ten and then you'll see..."

Rupert and the others look on dejectedly as the Jester reappears, carrying the Fox brothers' prizes... "Custard pies!" he beams. "Baked to a special recipe and fit for a King." "Hurrah!" cheers Freddy. "A whole pie each, and none for anyone else!" "Absolutely!" declares the Jester. "These are all yours..." To everyone's surprise, he steps forward and throws the pies at the twins. "Richly deserved!" he laughs as they splutter in astonishment. "I'm sure your friends agree."

For once in their lives, Freddy and Ferdy are completely lost for words... "Why?" splutters Freddy at last. "I thought you liked our trick?" "I did!" says the Jester. "But rules are rules. It was past twelve o'clock when you ran off and left the others stranded..." While the Foxes wipe their faces with wet flannels, the Jester tells the others that he really has prepared a special feast. "Close your eyes and count to ten!" he calls. "Time for the Pranksters' party..."

RUPERT ENJOYS THE PARTY

He whisks the cloth clear to reveal
The table's laid. "Our Fool's Day meal!"

"Let's have another contest when
The first of April comes again!"

The Jester waves and calls goodbye –
"Till next year!" Rupert hears him cry.

The Fox twins say next time they're sure
They'll win the Jester's prize once more!

To Rupert's amazement, the Jester pulls away the cloth to reveal a splendid feast. "Real food this time!" he announces. "Take your places and eat your fill. No more pranks for the rest of the day, I promise..." As the chums tuck in, they talk about all the jokes they've played. "It was fun!" laughs Rupert. "I think we ought to have a Fool's Day Festival every year!" "I don't see why not!" nods the Jester. "I enjoyed myself too. Watching other people's pranks makes a welcome change!"

At the end of the party, the Jester tells the pals they have all won special prizes for being such good sports. "Here's to Nutwood's next Fool's Day Festival!" he calls as they set off through the maze. "What a lark!" says Freddy. "I like the idea of having another competition next year." "Me too!" smiles Ferdy. "We won't make the same mistake twice!" "No!" laughs Rupert. "But you *did* win first prize, even if it wasn't quite what you were expecting!"

THE END

RUPERT
and the
Rust Mites

John Harrold.

RUPERT GOES ON AN ERRAND

The snow has melted for the year –
It's time to get the garden clear...

"This old tin bucket's rusted through!"
"I'll take it to the tip for you..."

"Stop!" calls a voice. "That bucket's great!
Don't throw it out just yet, please wait..."

"The Professor wants things like these
To demonstrate his latest wheeze!"

The winter snow has melted in Nutwood and Mr. Bear is outside, working in the garden... "It's too early to plant anything!" he tells Rupert. "There might be a frost. The best thing we can do is tidy up all these twigs and fallen branches." Before they go indoors, the pair decide to sort out the garden shed. "This old bucket's too rusty to be any use," says Rupert's father. "I think the best thing would be to take it to the tip!" "I'll go!" says Rupert. "There might be something interesting there..."

Carrying the rusty bucket, Rupert sets off across the common towards Nutwood's tip. "The last time I came here was with Bingo, to look for old pram wheels to make a go-cart," he thinks. "I wonder what I'll find today?" The heap of metal objects is hidden behind a clump of bushes. As he gets nearer, Rupert spots an old bedstead, some rusty springs and a pram. He is just about to add his bucket to the pile when a voice calls out, "Stop! Wait a moment! That rusty pail is just what I need."

RUPERT VISITS THE PROFESSOR

*"I'll add your bucket to the rest
Then hurry back to start the test..."*

*"Test?" Rupert blinks. "Yes, come and see –
It won't take long, just follow me!"*

*"Well done!" the old Professor cries.
"We really needed fresh supplies!"*

*"Come on! My new machine's all set –
The best thing I've invented yet!"*

As Rupert looks round, Bodkin, the old Professor's servant, steps out from behind the tip. "Hello!" he smiles. "Sorry to startle you but I'm collecting old metal, like that bucket of yours." "Really?" blinks Rupert. "It's perfect!" laughs Bodkin. "The Professor's asked me to collect rusty objects for his latest experiment..." Chuckling at Rupert's surprise, he invites him to come and see what they are up to... "We're still at the early stages, but the Professor is very pleased at how it's going!"

As Rupert and Bodkin near the Professor's tower he waves out of a window, then comes running down to meet them. "Well done!" he beams. "More rusty metal for us to get to work on..." "What are you doing with it?" blinks Rupert. "Bodkin said you'd invented a new machine. Does it use old metal as fuel?" "Not exactly!" smiles the Professor. "I've tried to go one better than that! Come through to the laboratory and I'll give you a demonstration. You won't believe it, unless you see for yourself..."

RUPERT SEES A NEW MACHINE

*"The Rust Reverser! Leaves old tin
As shiny as a brand new pin!"*

*"To demonstrate what it can do
I'll test it on this old horseshoe..."*

*"I'll make the rust all vanish now –
Watch carefully and you'll see how!"*

*The rusty horseshoe starts to gleam,
Caught in a dazzling, silver beam...*

At the back of the laboratory, Rupert sees a strange new machine... "It's called the Rust Reverser," beams the Professor. "It turns back the clock and restores metal objects, like this old horseshoe, to their original condition." "Really?" blinks Rupert. "But that's amazing. It sounds like a magic spell!" "It looks like one too!" chuckles the Professor. "I couldn't believe my eyes when we finally did it! The process seems to work on anything that's rusty."

As Rupert looks on, the Professor places the old horseshoe on a fine mesh platform then pushes down a heavy lever... "Stand clear, everyone!" he calls. A beam of light shines down from above, bathing the whole platform in a silvery glow. "The horseshoe!" gasps Rupert. "It's glowing red-hot, just like a blacksmith's forge." "Exactly!" nods Bodkin. "But there's more to it than that! Wait till the Professor switches the Reverser off! That's when you'll see something really special..."

RUPERT IS AMAZED

"Amazing!" Rupert blinks. "It's true!
The horseshoe looks as good as new!"

"It works on any rusty find –
Bright gleaming metal's left behind!"

"This chamber holds the dislodged rust –
It looks just like a pile of dust!"

"We'll try your bucket now. Let's see
What it looks like when it's rust-free..."

After a few minutes, the Professor turns off the machine and waits for the horseshoe to cool down. "What do you think?" he asks. "Looks a bit different now, doesn't it?" "Amazing!" blinks Rupert. "It's all silver and shiny, just like new." "That's because I've removed the rust!" laughs the Professor. Behind the machine is a jumbled pile of more gleaming metal objects. "All from the tip!" smiles Nutwood's inventor. "They're still a bit dented, but not a trace of rust."

Rupert is amazed by the Professor's new machine, which seems to work by shaking all the rust loose. "Rust particles fall through the mesh and are gathered down below," explains the inventor. "You can see how busy we've been by looking inside!" Producing the bucket from Rupert's garden, Bodkin puts it on the platform for another demonstration. "All set?" asks the Professor. "Let's see what we can do!" He switches on the Reverser and waits until the bucket starts to glow...

RUPERT HAS AN EARLY CALLER

"The rust's gone, Rupert, but, oh, dear!
Your bucket's still worn through, I fear..."

"Thanks!" Rupert calls. "Your new machine
Must be the best I've ever seen!"

Early next morning, Mrs. Bear
Hears someone at the door. "Who's there?"

It's Bodkin. "I've been sent to bring
Rupert at once, to see something..."

"Oh, dear!" sighs the Professor as he looks at Rupert's bucket. "The rust has all gone, but I'm afraid it's still full of holes..." "Never mind," says Rupert. "It was very interesting to see your machine." "Early days, yet!" declares the Professor as Rupert sets off home. "I'd like to make a smaller version next. Imagine what would happen if everybody had one! No more rusting metal. We could stop it spreading at the very first sign. Think of all the metal we'd save. Things could last forever!"

Next morning, Rupert has just finished breakfast when he hears someone knocking at the front door... "I wonder who's there?" says his mother. "Perhaps the Postman's brought us a parcel?" To Mrs. Bear's surprise, she finds Bodkin on the front step, gasping for breath... "Morning, Rupert!" he puffs. "Professor sent me over to fetch you. Something very odd has happened and he'd like you to come and see. Hope you don't mind, Mrs. Bear. It isn't dangerous. At least, I don't think so..."

RUPERT SEES WHAT HAS HAPPENED

"The Professor is safe and sound,
But mystified by what we've found..."

"The door to my laboratory
Fell off its hinges – as you see!"

"I can't explain what made it fall,
There's no-one in the lab at all."

As Rupert peers inside he's sure
He spots a rust mark on the floor...

Rupert hurries to the Professor's tower with Bodkin. "What's wrong?" he asks. "Is it anything to do with the new machine?" "Might be!" nods the inventor's servant. "We don't know yet. You'll see for yourself, when we get there. All very strange, if you ask me!" When Rupert arrives, he finds the Professor staring at the door to his laboratory, which lies hanging off its hinges. "Goodness!" blinks Rupert. "Has there been a break in?" "No!" says the Professor. "It's more like a break out!"

"It's very odd!" says the Professor. "Look at the way the door has fallen..." "Outwards, as if someone had pushed it from inside!" blinks Rupert. "Exactly!" nods his friend. "The strange thing is, there's nobody there! The lab was empty last night, when I locked up, and it seems to be empty now..." Rupert peers through the doorway into the cluttered room. Everything appears to be completely normal, except for a rusty-coloured trail which leads towards the Professor's new machine...

33

RUPERT FINDS A CLUE

"The new machine! It's damaged too!
Just like the hinges – rusted through!"

"Bless me! You're right, Rupert! What's more
The rust's all vanished from the store..."

A rusty trail's the only clue –
"How strange! It seems to be brand new!"

Then, suddenly, they hear a sound –
Another door falls to the ground!

Rupert follows the trail across the laboratory to the Rust Reverser. "Look!" he cries. "There's a hole in the side of the machine. It's rusted right through." "Bless me!" blinks the Professor. "Perhaps there's a side-effect I hadn't thought of..." Opening the door of the rust chamber, he peers inside then gasps in amazement. "It's empty! The rust we shook loose yesterday has disappeared." "Not completely!" says Rupert. "Some of it's still scattered on the floor..."

Walking back through the laboratory, the startled friends follow the rusty trail downstairs. "I can't understand how it got here!" says the Professor. "If the machine blew up, I suppose the force might have wrecked the door and thrown all the rust into the air..." "Blown up?" says Bodkin. "I didn't hear any explosion. Only a crash as the door fell off..." As he speaks, there is a tremendous bang downstairs. "What was that?" blinks the Professor. "It sounded like *another* door!"

RUPERT FOLLOWS A SWARM

*"The **front** door now!" blinks Rupert. "Why?"*
He runs outside, then gives a cry...

"A swarm of ants! I'm sure I saw
Them run from underneath the door!"

"Quick, Rupert! Keep the swarm in sight –
Ants don't eat wood, but termites might..."

"My magnifying glass should show
Us everything we need to know..."

Hurrying down from the laboratory, Rupert and the Professor are amazed to find the front door lying in the path as if it has been pushed forward... "Astonishing!" blinks the Inventor. "I wonder what's caused that? Doors don't just fall off their hinges!" The pair peer out into the garden, but there is nobody there. "Look at the path!" gasps Rupert suddenly. "There's a great swarm of ants..." "Ants?" blinks the Professor. "Bless me! I think you're right. It looks like a whole colony!"

"How extraordinary!" cries the Professor. "I've never seen a swarm like it..." "Do you suppose they're anything to do with the door?" asks Rupert. "They might be," shrugs the Professor. "Perhaps some sort of wood-eating termite?" Taking a magnifying glass from his pocket, he hurries after the insects, to take a closer look. "This could be serious!" he declares. "There might be an infestation. Insects that swarm like this are normally on the look-out for a new home!"

RUPERT SEES THE RUST MITES

"Good, gracious!" the Professor cries.
"Rust mites! Now that is a surprise…"

"They live on metal! Normally
They're quite impossible to see!"

"The swarm of rust mites must have been
All shaken loose by my machine!"

"They'll stay together 'till they find
More rusty metal of some kind…"

Kneeling down by the side of the path, the Professor peers through his magnifying glass and gives a cry of amazement. "Rupert! They're not ants at all! These are rust mites…" "Rust mites?" blinks Rupert. "Look," says the Professor, handing him the glass. Rupert has never seen anything like the tiny brown creatures marching along the path. "They eat rusty metal!" explains the Professor. "It's very rare to see them out in the open. They're normally so well camouflaged they're impossible to see…"

"I didn't think of mites when I invented the Reverser," admits the Professor. "I suppose they've been shaken loose from all the rusty metal we've used…" "They must have broken out of the laboratory!" blinks Rupert. "First they ate through the side of the machine, then they gnawed the hinges of the door!" "Amazing, isn't it?" nods the inventor. "I suppose they're on the look-out for more rusty metal to eat!" "It's like a swarm of locusts!" gasps Rupert. "What will they do next?"

RUPERT TELLS HIS PARENTS

*"Don't worry! They'll soon find a tin
Or rusty tub to settle in..."*

*"I hope he's right! Imagine what
They might get up to if he's not..."*

*Rupert runs home again to tell
His parents of the mites as well...*

*"A swarm?" blinks Mr. Bear. "Oh, dear!
I hope they won't cause trouble here!"*

To Rupert's surprise, the Professor doesn't seem very worried about the swarm of mites... "They'll soon find more rusty metal," he says. "It's only because we shut them in a box that they gathered in a swarm. As soon as they've spread out you won't even notice they're there." "I suppose he's right!" thinks Rupert as he hurries home for lunch. "It's a good job they only eat old metal! Imagine what would happen if they started attacking new things too..."

As soon as Rupert gets home, he tells his parents all about the rust mites and how they escaped from the Professor's laboratory... "Rust mites?" blinks Mr. Bear. "I've never heard of them!" "Neither have I," says his wife. "I hope they're not dangerous!" "The Professor doesn't think so," explains Rupert. "He says they only attack rusty old metal." "That's all right then!" laughs Mr. Bear. "So long as they don't start munching their way through any of Nutwood's motor cars..."

RUPERT SPOTS A STRANGER

Next morning, Rupert hurries out
To see if his chums are about...

A figure lumbers into sight –
"It looks just like an armoured knight!"

"It's coming this way!" Rupert blinks.
"I'll hide behind a tree!" he thinks...

The rusty knight goes clanking by –
"I wonder where he's bound, and why?"

Next morning, Rupert decides to go for a walk on Nutwood common. "I wonder if any of the others will be there?" he thinks. "Bill's new kite would be fun to fly, if there's enough wind..." As he climbs to the top of the hill, Rupert suddenly hears a strange clanking noise. "What's that?" he blinks. "It sounds like a machine that needs oiling! "To his astonishment, he spots a far-off figure dressed in a suit of armour, like an old-fashioned knight. "Who can it be?" he thinks...

As Rupert stands watching the armoured figure he suddenly realises that it is clanking its way towards him. Hiding behind a tree, he waits until it passes, then peers out to get a closer view... To his surprise, the knight's rusty armour seems to be made up of old tin cans. On its tunic, the clanking figure has a strange sign, which is oddly familiar. At first, Rupert can't think where he has seen it before, but as the knight marches on he suddenly knows. "Rust mites!" he blinks.

RUPERT FOLLOWS THE KNIGHT

"The old Professor's! Now I see –
He's from the rust mites! Goodness me!"

Drawing a rusty sword, he knocks
Upon the door's hinges and locks.

The knight then ceases his attack
Upon the door and stands well back...

He clanks inside. "What shall I do?"
Thinks Rupert as he enters too.

"I wonder where he's going?" thinks Rupert as the rusty knight marches briskly across the common. Keeping out of sight, he follows at a distance and soon learns the answer to his question... "The old Professor's tower!" he gasps. "The mites must have told him all about the new machine. I'd better warn the Professor!" Hurrying to the tower, Rupert finds that Nutwood's inventor is not at home. Crouching down behind a bush, he watches the knight take a sword from his belt and strike the door.

Shortly after the knight's sword touches the door, it falls down with a mighty crash. "He must have rusted through the hinges!" gasps Rupert. "The sword's like a magic wand!" Clanking forward, the armoured figure crosses the makeshift drawbridge and enters the Professor's tower. "I wonder what he'll do when he finds there's nobody in?" thinks Rupert. "I could go and fetch P.C. Growler, but it might be too late by then..." Creeping silently over the fallen door he follows the knight inside.

RUPERT SAVES THE NEW MACHINE

The knight climbs stiffly up the stairs –
Can Rupert catch him unawares?

"The new machine!" blinks Rupert. "Wait!"
The knight turns with a look of hate.

"Why should I spare this dread machine?
The worse device I've ever seen!"

The Professor arrives to see
The knight in his laboratory...

Climbing stiffly upstairs, the knight heads straight for the Professor's laboratory, leaving a trail of rust mites behind it as it goes... "Of course!" thinks Rupert. "They must have been leading him to the Professor's new device! That explains how he found it so quickly." As Rupert enters the lab he sees the knight standing over the Rust Reverser with his sword already drawn. "Stop!" he calls. "Don't destroy the Professor's machine. It's one of his best inventions..." The knight turns to Rupert with an angry stare.

"Spare this machine?" it croaks. "Never! My people have told me of its purpose. To rob them of their homes, deny them nature's bounty and imprison them. I have come to free them from its tyranny..." As he speaks the Professor appears in the doorway, blinking in astonishment at the unexpected visitor. "Dear me!" he gasps. "Who are you? Why have you broken into my laboratory?" "Yours!" snarls the knight. "So you are the fiend I have come to vanquish!"

40

RUPERT HEARS THE KNIGHT'S TALE

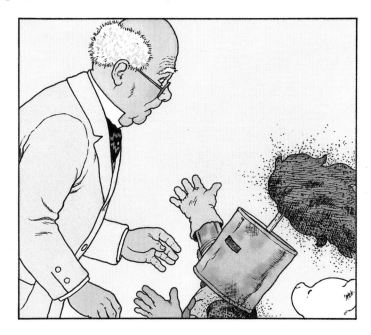

"Professor!" calls the angry knight.
"Let me explain my people's plight..."

"If things don't rust, we'll starve and die –
Your work will be the reason why..."

"Wait!" Rupert smiles. "I think I know
A place where all the mites can go..."

"From now on, I can promise we
Will let things rust quite naturally!"

"Fiend?" blinks the Professor. "Steady on! I'm sure there's a mistake..." "What else should I call the inventor of this infernal machine!" replies the knight. "My people were right to be alarmed. It threatens our whole way of life." "Oh, dear," sighs the Professor. "I see... I have to admit I never thought of rust from your point of view." "That's why your machine is so dangerous!" says the Knight. "Reversing rust might help you but for us it means starvation, doom and disaster!"

"So the rust mites are hungry..." says Rupert. "I know where there's lots of rusty metal they can have." "And I agree to stop my experiments!" adds the Professor hurriedly. "It was a nice idea, but I see now that metal must rust, just as wood rots and rain falls from the sky..." "Good!" nods the knight. "Then I shall leave you in peace." "I'll show you where the metal is," says Rupert. "There's plenty left on Nutwood's tip." "Bravo!" beams the Professor, shaking hands with the rust mites' champion.

RUPERT MAKES AMENDS

The knight agrees to come and see
Where the rust mites' new home might be...

"The tip!" says Rupert. "Every day
New metal things are thrown away!"

"A perfect new home!" says the knight.
"There's no more need for us to fight..."

"Good!" Bodkin smiles. "Just goes to show
How things turn out – you never know..."

Moments later, a strange procession crosses Nutwood common, with Rupert leading the way and the rusty knight clanking along behind him. The old Professor comes next, followed by Bodkin, with a cart full of left-over junk. "This is the perfect place for rusty metal!" says Rupert, pointing to Nutwood's tip. "Nobody will disturb the mites and they'll always have a fresh supply of food." "It looks perfect!" laughs the knight. "With a home like this, my people will be safe once more..."

"Thank you!" says the knight. "The rust mites will not forget this kindness from the people of Nutwood. With riches in such abundance, we can cease our restless search and spare more of your metal possessions..." Leaving him to summon the rust mites, Rupert and the Professor start back towards the tower, with Bodkin pushing the empty cart. "Less rust, eh?" he chuckles. "It seems your invention wasn't wasted after all, Professor! Just shows how things have a funny way of turning out..."

RUPERT
and the
Strawberries

John Harrold.

RUPERT AND EDWARD GO HIKING

One sunny morning Rupert hears
The doorbell. "Edward Trunk!" he cheers...

The two chums have agreed that they
Will go out hiking for the day.

"A map to guide us there and back –
Your compass will show the right track..."

"We'll take this path, then stop to see
Which way our final route should be."

It is a sunny morning in Nutwood and Rupert is up bright and early, getting ready to go on a hike with Edward Trunk... "You've certainly picked a nice day!" smiles Mrs. Bear as she helps him pack some sandwiches. "There isn't a cloud in the sky." Just then, the doorbell rings. "Hello!" beams Edward. "I hope I'm not too early?" "No!" laughs Rupert. "Come in while I finish getting ready. It won't take long. Dad's just looking out a map. He's got one that shows the whole of Nutwood..."

When Rupert's father appears with the map, Edward shows him the compass he had for his birthday. "Excellent!" says Mr. Bear. "It's just the thing to take on a walk. With a map and compass you should be able to work out exactly where you are." "Where shall we go?" asks Edward as the pair set out. "Up to the hills or down to the lake?" "The edge of the common!" says Rupert. "We can stop to look at the map when we get there." "Good!" says Edward. "I can use my compass too..."

RUPERT HEARS SOMETHING IS WRONG

"There's Gaffer Jarge's house. He'll know
Which way the best footpaths all go..."

The old man gives a sudden cry –
The chums both run to find out why...

Old Gaffer Jarge explains that he
Has uncovered a robbery!

"My strawberry plants have been stripped bare.
There's not one left!" he tells the pair.

As the pals make their way along the lane, they come to Gaffer Jarge's house by the edge of the common. "I wonder if he's in?" says Rupert. "He might be able to point out some good walks on our map. Gaffer Jarge knows all the paths round Nutwood..." The pair spot the old man, standing outside in his garden. To their surprise, he stares intently at the ground, then gives a cry of despair. "Something's wrong!" blinks Rupert. "We'd better see if he needs help!"

"Hello, young 'uns!" says Gaffer Jarge. "Sorry if I startled you but I've just discovered a robbery!" "Burglars?" gasps Rupert. "I'll fetch P.C. Growler!" "No!" sighs the old man. "'Tis not my house that's been robbed. 'Tis my garden..." Leading the chums to the side of the house, Gaffer Jarge points to a neatly tended vegetable plot. "What's wrong?" blinks Edward. "It all looks fine to me..." "Strawberries!" says Jarge. "All the ripe ones I've been saving for Nutwood's Summer Fête!"

RUPERT MEETS HORACE HEDGEHOG

*"A strawberry thief! Now nobody
Can have a Nutwood strawberry tea…"*

*"Hello!" says Horace. "You two should
Look for wild berries, in the wood…"*

*"Strawberries?" Rupert blinks. "I'm sure
I've never found them wild before…"*

*"Look carefully! They're very small –
Most folk don't notice them at all!"*

"I wonder who can have stolen all the strawberries from Gaffer Jarge's garden?" says Edward as the pals resume their walk. "It means there won't be any strawberry teas at this year's village fête!" As the pair cross the common they suddenly hear a rustling sound from the nearby bushes. "Horace!" calls Rupert. "How nice to see you! Edward and I are just off for a walk." "Did someone mention strawberries?" asks the little hedgehog. "There are plenty in the woods, if you know where to look…"

"Strawberries in the woods?" blinks Rupert. "I've often seen blackberries in the hedgerows, but I've never even thought of looking for anything else…" "You'll find them there if you search carefully enough!" laughs Horace. "They're much smaller than garden strawberries but well worth searching out. Woodland creatures like me find all sorts of berries growing in the woods. Birds like them too, you know. Especially strawberries! They seem to be their favourite fruit!"

RUPERT STUDIES THE MAP

*The pals search in amongst the trees
But still can't find the strawberries...*

*At last they give up in despair –
"The berries could be anywhere!"*

*The chums have lunch and look to see
How far from Nutwood they should be.*

*"Look, Berry Down! It's just a name
But let's look there next, all the same..."*

Following Horace Hedgehog's directions, Rupert and Edward enter the woods and start searching for wild strawberries... "I can't see any!" shrugs Edward. "Neither can I!" admits Rupert. "Perhaps they've all been eaten by birds?" The chums are both feeling hungry by now and agree to stop for their picnic before going any further. "It's all very well for Horace!" says Edward. "He knows the forest better than anyone else in Nutwood! We could be searching for hours and still not find any berries..."

As Rupert and Edward eat their sandwiches, they decide to look at Mr. Bear's map of Nutwood. "I think we should give up searching for strawberries and continue our walk," suggests Edward. Rupert agrees and begins to look carefully at all the forest paths. "There's a bridge over the river here," he starts, then breaks off with a sudden cry. "Berry Down!" he gasps, pointing at the map. "Look, Edward! I'm sure it's where Horace Hedgehog meant us to search..."

Edward says his compass will show
Which way the two chums have to go...

"That clearing looks to be the spot –
Let's find out if we're right or not."

"A bramble patch! That must be why
It's Berry Down!" the two chums sigh.

A little bird flies down. "I know
Where lots of wild strawberries grow!"

Before the pals set out, Edward checks the direction on the map then works out the way by using his compass... "This is fun!" he laughs. "I was hoping we'd have some proper pathfinding to do!" The pair keep going in the same direction until they leave the wood and cross a grassy clearing. "This doesn't look right," sighs Edward. "There aren't any berries here either!" "Look!" says Rupert. "What about those brambles? Berry Down must be on the far side. Let's take a closer look..."

When the chums reach the clearing they are disappointed to find there are still no wild strawberries to be seen... "Only brambles!" says Rupert. "I suppose it must be called Berry Down because of all the blackberries..." Just then, a little bird flies up from the bushes and flaps its wings excitedly. "Too early to start gathering blackberries yet!" it chirps. "But I know where lots of strawberries grow, if that's what you're after! Follow me and I'll show you where to look."

RUPERT FINDS WILD STRAWBERRIES

"This way!" the bird chirps. "Follow me!
Squeeze through the brambles carefully..."

The two pals marvel in surprise –
Unable to believe their eyes...

Edward begins to fill his pack
With strawberries to carry back...

"Stop!" cries an Imp of Spring. "We grew
Those strawberries. They're not for you!"

To the chums' surprise, the little bird flies up to a gap in the brambles. "This way!" it calls. "You'll have to push your way through! Be careful you don't get prickled..." Rupert is the first to emerge on the other side of the bramble hedge. "Amazing!" he calls. "There's a whole field of strawberries! Come and see..." Edward can hardly fit through the gap, but with a determined shove he enters the hidden field and blinks in disbelief. "It almost looks like somebody's garden..."

Delighted at their find, Rupert and Edward decide to take some strawberries home. "We can come back and pick more for the village fête!" says Rupert. "There are so many here, I'm sure there'll be enough..." "Delicious!" says Edward, filling his rucksack with the tiny red berries. "It's amazing to find so many growing wild." As he speaks, the chums hear an angry cry. It is one of Nutwood's Imps of Spring... "Stop!" he calls. "This garden is private. What do you mean by stealing *our* fruit?"

RUPERT IS SCOLDED BY IMPS

The Imp blows on a whistle for
Two guards who lift a hidden door...

They lead the two pals underground –
"The King must see this proof we've found!"

The pals are taken down to where
The Imps' King waits to see the pair.

He spots the berries straightaway
And asks what Rupert has to say...

Before the chums can say anything, the Imp blows a shrill note on a tiny silver whistle. A hidden trap-door opens and two more Imps appear... "Strawberry thieves!" declares the first Imp. "I caught them red-handed, with bags full of fruit!" "Please," stammers Rupert. "We didn't mean to steal anything. Edward and I thought the strawberries were wild." "Come with us!" demands the sentry. "The King should hear a case like this. We'll take your bags as evidence and see what he decides..."

The Imps lead the chums along a narrow passage that twists and turns deeper and deeper underground. Eventually they come to a rocky chamber which houses the King's throne. "Strawberry thieves!" announces the guard. "Found picking berries in the middle of the wood. Admitted the charge but claimed it was all a mistake..." "Rupert!" gasps the Imps' King. "Can this be true? Tell me how you came to be gathering fruit so deep in the woods. Berry Down is out of bounds to all except Imps."

RUPERT IS FORGIVEN

The King hears how a thief has struck
at Nutwood's Fête. "What rotten luck!"

He says the pals can have some more
Strawberries from the Imps' own store.

"My guards will try to help you stop
The thief who's raiding Nutwood's crop."

"Come on!" they call. "We'll try to find
What clues the thief has left behind..."

The Imps' King listens carefully as Rupert explains all about the strawberries that went missing from Gaffer Jarge's garden... "We were only trying to find some more for the village fête," says Rupert. "I'd no idea they belonged to you." "No harm done!" smiles the King. "To show there are no hard feelings, I've decided to give you some extra strawberries to take back to Nutwood for Gaffer Jarge. My guards will try to help you find the real strawberry thief too."

As one of the Imps goes to fetch extra fruit for the pals, the King gets Rupert to tell his guards about the strawberries that vanished from Gaffer Jarge's garden... "We'd better go with you and search for clues!" says the first of the sentries. His companion runs off to get a large net. "This might come in useful if we find the thief," he says. "Good luck!" calls their King. "A berry thief in Nutwood's gardens might endanger all our crops. I'm relying on you to put things right..."

RUPERT RETURNS WITH STRAWBERRIES

The two chums are surprised to see
Some steps beneath a hollow tree...

The pals climb out, amazed at how
They're nearly back in Nutwood now.

The pair show Gaffer Jarge their prize –
"More strawberries! Bless me!" he cries.

"They're from the Imps!" says Rupert. "We
Told them about your robbery..."

The Imps seem quite excited at having a mystery to solve. "We'll start at the scene of the crime!" declares the first. "The thief must have a taste for strawberries. Perhaps we can use some of ours to bait a trap..." To the pals' surprise, the path from the throne room ends in a steep flight of steps under a large, hollow tree. Opening a door, the Imps step out on to a grassy clearing, which Rupert recognises at once. "Gaffer Jarge's cottage!" he gasps. "We've taken a short cut!"

Gaffer Jarge is still in his garden as Rupert and Edward appear, each carrying a basket full of tiny strawberries. "Bless me!" he blinks. "Wherever did you find those?" "In the woods!" laughs Rupert and is about to explain, when the old man suddenly catches sight of the two chums' companions... "Imps!" he gasps. "First time I've ever seen 'em in Nutwood! Keep to the woods as a rule." "We met them in the woods while we were looking for strawberries," explains Rupert. "They've come to help us catch the thief!"

RUPERT HELPS TO CATCH A THIEF

*The Imps and Rupert plan to catch
The thief by watching Gaffer's patch...*

*"Listen!" says Edward. "I can hear
The bushes rustling somewhere near!"*

*The chums peer out, amazed to see
The Imps creep forward silently.*

*They throw their net and trap the thief
Who starts to struggle underneath...*

While Gaffer Jarge takes the baskets of fruit indoors, Rupert shows the Imps the old man's strawberry patch... "Perfect!" nods the first. "We'll sprinkle a few of our berries round the edge, then everyone can keep watch to see if the thief returns." Rupert and Edward take cover as the Imps bait their trap. For a long time nothing happens, then Edward gives a sudden start. "Listen, Rupert! I can hear somebody pushing their way through the bushes..."

Rupert and Edward peer out from their hiding place towards the rustling hedge. "There's definitely someone there!" hisses an Imp. "We're going to try to catch them by surprise..." Creeping forward, the pair lift their net high in the air, then drop it over the bushes with a cry of triumph. "Hurrah!" calls Edward. "You've done it!" "Stop struggling!" demands the second Imp. "You won't get away, you know. Step into the garden and explain what you mean by taking Gaffer Jarge's strawberries!"

RUPERT SOLVES THE MYSTERY

The chums both look on anxiously –
Who can the strawberry thief be?

"We've caught a donkey!" Rupert cries.
"So you're the thief - what a surprise!"

"Goodness!" laughs Gaffer. "Now I see
What's happened. It's just Strawberry!"

"That's what she's called!" he tells the pair.
"My nephew's brought her for the Fair!"

The captive makes no reply but pushes forward, towards the chums. "It looks too big to be a person!" blinks Edward. "You're right!" nods Rupert. "I think we must have caught an animal..." The Imps look nervously at the net, then start to lift a corner. "What if it's from the zoo?" whispers one. "It might be a lion, or a tiger..." "A donkey!" laughs Rupert as a shaggy head peeps out. "So *you're* the strawberry thief! But where have you come from? Whatever are you doing in Nutwood?"

When Gaffer Jarge spots the donkey he gives a cry of surprise. "Goodness, lads! You've found her! Strawberry's been missing all day..." "Strawberry?" blinks Rupert. "Is that the donkey's name?" "It's what my nephew calls her," explains the old man. "He brought her to Nutwood for tomorrow's fête but the silly thing wandered off while nobody was looking!" "I didn't know that donkeys ate strawberries!" says Edward. "This one does!" laughs Gaffer Jarge. "Has done ever since she was a foal..."

RUPERT HAS A DONKEY RIDE

*A young man calls her name and then
Sees that Strawberry's found again...*

*"At last!" he smiles. "I've searched all day!
She wandered off and lost her way!"*

*Jim thanks the Nutwood chums and then
Gives them a ride back home again.*

*"A donkey!" marvels Mrs. Bear
And welcomes back the lucky pair.*

As Gaffer Jarge stands talking to the chums, they hear a voice calling Strawberry's name... "My nephew, Jim!" says the old man and waves to show that the donkey has been found. "At last!" says Strawberry's owner. "I hope she hasn't been raiding everyone's gardens." "Only mine!" laughs his uncle. "But Rupert and Edward have found some more berries, so there's no harm done..." "Case solved!" says the Imps' leader. "I can tell the King that there's no more cause for alarm."

Gaffer Jarge's nephew is so pleased to have found Strawberry that he offers the chums a ride home. The Imps of Spring call goodbye, then the pair set off along the lane. As they near Rupert's cottage, Mrs. Bear peers over the gate and blinks in amazement at what she sees... "A donkey ride!" she gasps. "I thought the Summer Fête was tomorrow!" "It is!" laughs Rupert. "And, now we've solved the mystery of Gaffer's garden, there'll be plenty of strawberries for everyone!"

THE END

RUPERT and

It's harvest time and Rupert's chums
Work hard before bad weather comes...

It is late summer and Farmer Brown is cutting the last of his corn. Rupert and his chums are helping by tying up the sheaves and loading them on to a wagon... "Well done, lads!" puffs the farmer. "This is always the last field in Nutwood to be harvested. Marks the ends of summer, my old father used to say. I'm just glad to get it done before it rains!" When the cart has been loaded, he unpacks a picnic to thank the pals for their help.

the Harvest Moon

*"The last field's finished everyone…
Thanks, lads!" says Farmer Brown. "Well done!"*

*"Perhaps I'll be a farmer too!"
Says Bill. "There's always lots to do."*

When the picnic ends, Farmer Brown takes the loaded wagon back along the lane, while the pals walk home across the fields… "That was fun!" laughs Bill. "I like working on the farm." "Me too!" says Algy. "Although it's not so enjoyable when it rains!" As the chums stroll on, Rupert spots Odmedod the scarecrow… "His year's nearly over!" he thinks. "He normally spends the winter in the old barn. I'll just go and say goodbye before he disappears…"

*Then Rupert spots another friend
Whose year is nearly at an end…*

RUPERT TALKS TO ODMEDOD

"Hello!" says Rupert. "Did you see?
We've all been working busily..."

"Yes," smiles the scarecrow. "Autumn soon,
But first we'll have a harvest moon!"

"Come back and see the moon tonight –
It's clearer out here – nice and bright!"

"A harvest moon? They're how we know
That summer's ending, with a glow!"

"Hello, Rupert!" smiles the scarecrow. "You've been busy! I saw you all helping Farmer Brown..." "We've just finished," says Rupert. "It's been a lovely sunny day." "It has been fine!" agrees Odmedod. "Perfect weather for harvesting, though the best is yet to come..." "What do you mean?" asks Rupert. "A harvest moon!" declares the scarecrow. "Bright as day and hanging in the sky like a great ball! Most folk hardly notice it because they're all indoors. You have to be out here to see it properly..."

Odmedod's description of the harvest moon is so exciting that Rupert decides to try to see it for himself... "Come back and join me after supper!" suggests Odmedod. "I will!" calls Rupert and hurries home for tea. "Did you know it's going to be a harvest moon tonight?" he asks Mr. Bear. "A harvest moon?" blinks Rupert's father. "I suppose it must be the right time of year! Can't say I'd given it a lot of thought..." "There's no mistaking a harvest moon!" smiles Mrs. Bear.

RUPERT SEES THE HARVEST MOON

That evening, Rupert waits and then
Slips out to see his chum again...

"The moon is bright tonight!" he blinks.
"It's almost light as day!" he thinks.

"Hello!" smiles Odmedod. "All set?
The evening's hardly started yet..."

"This way..." the scarecrow gives a call.
"Look, Rupert! Can you see them all?"

When Rupert has finished supper, he slips outside and sets off towards Odmedod's field... "It's not very far," he thinks. "If I hurry, I should get there before it's too late." Away from the lights of the village, Rupert notices the silvery glow of the moon growing stronger and stronger. As he reaches the edge of the common he is amazed at how big the moon looks, hanging over the fields. "It's like the nursery rhyme," he blinks. "Girls and boys come out to play, the moon doth shine as bright as day..."

As Rupert crosses the common, he finds Odmedod waiting for him by the fence... "What do you think?" smiles the scarecrow. "Wonderful!" says Rupert. "I've never seen the moon shine so brightly!" "If you hurry, you'll see something even more special," promises Odmedod. "This way..." Following his friend, Rupert spots a flock of birds, wheeling and swooping over the newly harvested field. "That's not all!" he blinks as they get closer. "I can see figures moving too! The field is full of people!"

RUPERT MEETS A CORN DOLLY

"They're dancing!" Rupert blinks. "But who?"
"Corn dollies, straw men, others too..."

"The mice and birds have come to glean
Grain left from where the harvest's been..."

"The dancers visit every year,
This field's the last – that's why they're here!"

"Come on!" a dolly calls. "Join in!
The dancing's about to begin..."

Peering into the field, Rupert sees that the moving figures are dancers, who leap and twirl to the music of two strange-looking fiddlers... "Corn dollies and straw men!" laughs Odmedod. "They're celebrating the end of the summer!" "And the birds?" marvels Rupert. "Gleaning!" says the scarecrow. "They and the field-mice are taking their share of the harvest. All the grain the farmer leaves behind..." "Amazing!" blinks Rupert. "They're my friends!" laughs the scarecrow. "Come and say hello...".

As the dancers skip past, Odmedod explains that they come to Nutwood every year to mark the end of the harvest. "This is the last field!" he smiles. "Always has been, for as long as anyone can remember..." Just then, one of the corn dollies catches hold of Rupert's hand. "Come and join the dance!" she laughs. "We're going to sing 'John Barleycorn'." "I know that!" says Odmedod. "It's one of my favourites!" "Places please!" calls a straw man. "The music's about to start!"

RUPERT JOINS THE DANCE

The two chums hear the fiddlers play
Then the next dance gets underway...

A bird swoops down. "It's Rupert Bear!
I thought I recognised you there..."

At last the dance comes to an end –
Rupert bids farewell to his friend...

"I'd better go! It's getting late –
But what an evening! It was great!"

Rupert and Odmedod join a circle of dancers, who all stand waiting for the fiddlers to play. "Sir John!" calls one of the straw men and suddenly everyone starts to dance. "This is fun!" laughs Rupert. "Yes!" says Odmedod. "All you have to do is follow the others. They'll change direction soon and go the other way..." As the pair dance, a startled bird swoops down to take a closer look. "Rupert Bear!" it chirps. "Fancy you being here! Everyone else in Nutwood is tucked up in bed..."

When the dancing ends, Rupert thanks Odmedod but tells him he has to be getting back. "I'd better not stay out too late!" he says. "Off you go, then!" nods the scarecrow. "The moon's still bright enough to show the way. You'll be home before you know it..." "Thanks for asking me!" calls Rupert as he hurries off. "You're welcome!" laughs his chum. "It's a very special evening, you know. No-one else in Nutwood has ever seen the dancers. Not even Farmer Brown!"

As Rupert thinks of where he's been
He can't believe the sights he's seen...

He yawns and clambers into bed,
The tunes still playing in his head...

"Who's there?" blinks Rupert. Then he sees
A Dolly calling, "Wake up, please!"

"Quick!" calls the scarecrow. "Follow me
At once! It's an emergency..."

Still marvelling at the dance of the corn dollies, Rupert hurries back to Nutwood and up the garden path... "I'd never have believed it!" he laughs. "Fancy there being a special festival to mark the end of the harvest... I wonder if I'll be able to join in next year, as well?" By the time he climbs into bed, Rupert is so sleepy he feels that the whole evening might have been a dream. "If I shut my eyes I can still hear the fiddlers playing 'John Barleycorn!'" he smiles.

During the night, Rupert dreams about the harvest moon and all the twirling dancers. He can hear them whoop and cry, calling his name over and over again... Suddenly he realises that the cry is coming from inside his room! "Rupert!" calls one of the dollies. "Wake up! Wake up! We need your help!" Jumping out of bed, Rupert hurries to the open window and peers into the garden. "Thank goodness!" calls Odmedod. "There's an emergency at Farmer Brown's! You're our only hope..."

RUPERT SEES THE SMOULDERING HAY

"A fire has broken out, I'm sure,
We saw smoke rising from the straw!"

"You're right!" says Rupert. "I see too!
Let's run and see what we can do..."

"There's nothing for it but to raise
The fire-brigade to fight the blaze..."

"A pump!" cries Rupert. "I think we
Can stop the fire immediately!"

Pulling on his clothes, Rupert hurries outside to join the scarecrow... "There's a fire!" gasps Odmedod. "We noticed it just as the dancers were leaving. It's the hay wain in the courtyard. The hot sun must have set it off. It's only smouldering at the moment but it could burst into flames at any moment..." As Rupert runs across the fields towards the farm he can see a thin wisp of smoke rising in the air. "Quickly!" he calls. "We might just be in time. There isn't a moment to lose."

By the time that Rupert reaches the farm, the smouldering wagon has started to burn more fiercely... "Too late!" wails Odmedod. "We'll have to call the fire brigade. The harvest will be lost by the time they arrive." "If we can put the fire out quickly we might be able to save it!" says Rupert. "The old pump in the courtyard still works, doesn't it?" "Yes," nods the scarecrow. "I suppose it's worth a try... If we can find a bucket!" "A bucket!" blinks Rupert. "There must be one nearby..."

RUPERT HAS AN IDEA

The dolly calls, "Look what I've found –
A bucket, lying on the ground..."

But as they go to fill the pail
They see their plan is bound to fail...

"The barn!" says Rupert. "Let's try there!"
"No use!" his friend cries in despair...

But Rupert laughs and gives a grin –
"I know! We'll use this tarpaulin!"

"Here!" calls the Corn Dolly. "I can see a bucket..." "Well done!" says Rupert. "I'll work the pump while you and Odmedod hold it in place." As he picks up the metal pail, Rupert gives a sudden groan. "Oh, no! This is no use, it's rusted through..." "That must be why Farmer Brown threw it away!" groans Odmedod. "We'll have to think of something else!" says Rupert. "Perhaps there's a hose-pipe hidden away in the barn? There must be something we can use to put out the fire..."

"I don't think you'll have any luck!" says Odmedod. "That barn's where I spend the winter. I'd have seen a hose if there was one. We might as well give up now." "I wonder?" murmurs Rupert. He looks thoughtfully at the barn then starts to pull out an old tarpaulin... "That's my eiderdown!" gasps Odmedod. "The farmer puts me under it every winter to keep out the damp!" "Exactly!" smiles Rupert. "It's waterproof! Just the right thing to keep water in!"

"I need the birds to help us too –
Please bring all your friends back with you..."

"Now, help me lay the sheet out flat
Beneath the pump, just like a mat..."

The birds fly back – "Please gather round
And form a circle on the ground..."

"Now hold the edge and start to fly,
Lift up the sheet – you'll soon see why!"

Odmedod and the Corn Dolly are mystified by Rupert's plan... How can a tarpaulin be what they need to get water to the burning wagon? "No time to explain!" says Rupert. "But I'll need all the birds from the cornfield to come and help us..." "Right you are!" chirps one of Odmedod's friends. "I'll fly off and fetch the others." "Help me lay this out now!" calls Rupert. "It has to be flat by the time the birds arrive..." "Here they come!" calls Odmedod. "I can see the whole flock!"

As the birds fly into the farmyard, Rupert asks them to form a big circle round the old tarpaulin. "I want you to lift it into the air!" he explains. "If you each grip the edge, you should be able to fly up with it in your claws." The birds hop round the tarpaulin and take their places. "Good!" calls Rupert. "Now let's see if you can hover in mid-air..." As the birds flap their wings, the tarpaulin slowly rises from the ground. "Well done!" cheers Rupert. "Just hold it there while I work the pump..."

RUPERT PUTS OUT THE FIRE

As Rupert pumps he starts to fill
The sheet the birds are holding still…

"We're ready now! Everything's set –
Please fly as high as you can get!"

The birds all hover. "That's good! Stop!
It's time to let the water drop…"

The sudden downpour does the trick
And soon puts out the burning rick.

Seizing the handle of the pump, Rupert starts to push it up and down as fast as he can. At first nothing happens, then a trickle of water appears… "Keep going!" urges Odmedod. "It's probably a bit rusty!" Sure enough, the pump soon gurgles into life, filling the tarpaulin like a huge canvas bucket. "That should be enough!" calls Rupert. "Now I want you to fly up over the burning wagon." The birds struggle with their heavy load, but slowly rise, higher and higher…

With the Nutwood birds all flapping their wings and pulling together, the bulging tarpaulin is soon hoisted high into the night sky, until it hovers above the smouldering wagon. "That's perfect!" calls Rupert, directing the fire-fighters from the courtyard below. "You can let go now…" The birds immediately release their load, which drenches the burning hay in a sudden downpour. "Hurrah!" cries Rupert. "That should do the trick. It's even better than a hose-pipe!"

RUPERT KEEPS OUT OF SIGHT

"It worked!" the Dolly cries. "Hurray!
We've rescued all the farmer's hay."

Just then, an upstairs light appears –
Farmer Brown must have heard their cheers...

"What's going on?" the Farmer cries.
"It must have been a dream!" he sighs.

"Well done!" smiles Odmedod. "I'm sure
That I'm the only one he saw..."

"Bravo!" calls Odmedod. "The fire's gone out!" "You did it!" cries the Corn Dolly, excitedly. "The harvest is saved!" "The birds did all the work!" says Rupert. "I was worried the water might be too heavy for them to lift..." "Three cheers for them too!" cries Odmedod. As the chums are celebrating, they suddenly see a light go on in one of the farmhouse windows. "Farmer Brown!" gasps Odmedod. "He must have been woken by all the noise. Quick, Rupert! Out of sight..."

Rupert and the Corn Dolly hide behind the wagon just as Farmer Brown peers out of the window into the courtyard. "What's going on?" he asks. Nobody answers and all he can see is Odmedod, standing still as a statue... "Must have been dreaming!" he murmurs at last. "Phew!" gasps the scarecrow. "That was close! He'd never understand what we'd all been doing, dancing in the moonlight..." "I suppose not," smiles Rupert. "And we have helped save his hay!"

RUPERT GOES BACK TO BED

The danger's past. "I'd better go –
I should be fast asleep, you know!"

"It's so late, it will soon be dawn!"
Thinks Rupert with a sleepy yawn.

"I've made the breakfast, sleepy head!
It's time that you were out of bed..."

"You should have seen the moon last night –
I've never seen it shine so bright!"

Now that the blaze has been safely extinguished, Odmedod and the Corn Dolly go back to join the others. "I'd better be getting back too!" says Rupert. "The moon's still bright, but it must be very late." As Rupert gets ready for bed, he is so sleepy that he can hardly stop yawning. "What an evening!" he marvels. "I never dreamt that gathering the corn would be such an adventure!" Climbing into bed he can still see the dancing figures, whirling and twirling as the fiddlers play...

Next morning, Rupert is so tired that he oversleeps and is still dozing soundly when his mother comes in to call him for breakfast... "You're very sleepy today!" she says. "Normally, you're up with the birds!" "I was..." murmurs Rupert as he thinks of how they helped him put out the fire. "You should have seen the harvest moon last night!" says Mrs. Bear. "It was so bright and full, it looked like a silvery sun..." "I...I think that sounds wonderful!" smiles Rupert.

RUPERT
and the
Smokescreen

John Harrold.

RUPERT'S PAL BUYS SOME FIREWORKS

*It's Autumn, and the time of year
When Bonfire Night is drawing near...*

*The pals crowd round excitedly
To see what fireworks there will be.*

*"There's Tigerlily! Let's see what
Is in the bag that she has got..."*

*"Smoke cones!" she smiles. "They're for a spell -
You need the magic words as well..."*

It is autumn in Nutwood. The trees are losing their leaves, the nights are drawing in and Rupert and his chums are looking forward to Bonfire Night... "Mr. Chimp's got some wonderful fireworks," says Willie Mouse. "I'm saving up to buy a big rocket!" "I like Roman candles!" smiles Ottoline. "Much nicer than those noisy bangers..." "Catherine wheels!" smiles Rupert. "They're my favourites!" "We'd better start building the bonfire," says Podgy. "It takes ages to gather everything together..."

The chums are still peering at the fireworks, when they see Tigerlily, leaving the shop with a big bag... "Hello!" calls Rupert. "You've made an early start this year. Bonfire Night isn't for a couple of weeks yet!" "Oh, these aren't for Guy Fawkes," says Tigerlily. "They're smoke cones, for one of my father's conjuring tricks." "Are they magic?" asks Ottoline. "Only when you make a spell!" smiles Tigerlily. "I'll show you, if you like. I'm sure my father won't mind!"

RUPERT WATCHES A DISPLAY

The chums are promised a display -
"Come!" Tigerlily calls. "This way..."

She takes six cones and makes a row -
"Good! Now it's time to start the show..."

The cones start smoking, red and blue
Then change to green and yellow too...

"The rainbow smoke is just for fun!
To let you know the show's begun..."

Carrying the cones carefully, Tigerlily leads the chums across the common, to a wide, open space... "This will be perfect!" she smiles. "You wait there, while I get things ready." "I wonder what she's up to?" whispers Podgy. "A spell of some sort!" says Willie. "I hope it isn't dangerous..." "Smoke cones sound pretty!" says Ottoline. "I expect they'll be different colours." As the chums look on, Tigerlily takes six cones and lays them in a straight line. "Nearly ready!" she calls.

The chums look on expectantly as Tigerlily strikes a match and lights each of the cones. "They're red!" says Willie. "Blue!" calls Bill. "Green!" cries Ottoline. "The colour keeps on changing!" laughs Rupert. "It's like a rainbow!" The fireworks fill the air with thick smoke, which rises in a billowing cloud. "All set!" calls Tigerlily. "I'll need a volunteer from the audience now. The coloured smoke is only a beginning. The real trick needs a spell to make it work..."

RUPERT'S CHUM BILL VANISHES

"I'll help!" Bill calls. "Now what's the trick?"
"Just walk to where the smoke looks thick!"

As Tigerlily speaks in rhyme
She waves her wand at the same time...

The chums watch Bill step through the smoke.
"He's only hiding! It's a joke..."

"No!" Willie gasps. "He isn't here -
You've made Bill Badger disappear!"

"I'll help with the trick!" says Bill. "What do you want me to do?" "I'm going to make you disappear!" smiles Tigerlily. "Really?" gasps Willie. "Yes!" says the Conjurer's daughter. "Watch carefully and he'll vanish before your eyes..." As Bill steps forward, Tigerlily explains she wants him to walk straight towards the smoking cones. Producing a wand from her sleeve, she waves it once and begins to chant a spell. "Prepare to travel, through the screen, where things go when they can't be seen..."

"Keep going!" calls Tigerlily as Bill reaches the wall of coloured smoke. "Step through to the other side..." "It's a trick!" whispers Podgy. "The smoke's too thick for us to see if Bill's there or not!" "Step round and see," smiles Tigerlily. "It's a trick all right, but a magic one, using a real spell." "He...he's really gone!" cries Willie Mouse. "Vanished!" blinks Ottoline. "Amazing!" gasps Rupert. "I was sure we'd find Bill standing on the other side of the cones!"

RUPERT SEES A SPELL FAIL

"But where's Bill gone?" "He's in Between!
Where things go when they can't be seen..."

"Don't worry! The next words I say
Will bring him back here straightaway..."

"Something's gone wrong! This spell of mine
Won't bring Bill back - there's not a sign..."

"I'm sorry! I don't understand...
He must be stuck in Between Land!"

"So, if Bill has vanished, where has he gone?" asks Rupert. "To Between Land!" smiles Tigerlily. "It's where conjurers always send things when they make them disappear." "Like watches?" blinks Willie. "I saw one of those vanish once." "That's right!" nods Tigerlily. "Silk handkerchiefs, thimbles, playing cards, even their assistants sometimes..." Waving her wand again, she recites a spell to bring Bill back. "Return to Nutwood now my friend. The magic trick is at an end."

Rupert and his chums peer into the smoke, all looking for a sign of Bill... "He's not there!" says Ottoline. "No!" blinks Tigerlily. "I...I don't think the spell can have worked." "Does that mean Bill's stuck in Between Land?" asks Rupert. "I'm afraid so!" nods his friend. "I can't understand what's wrong! I'm sure I remembered the right words. The spell should have brought him back to Nutwood straightaway." "What are we going to do *now*?" asks Willie. "We can't just leave Bill stranded!"

RUPERT GOES TO FIND BILL

"We'll have to wait, till later, when
My father comes back home again..."

"No!" Rupert says. "I'll go and see
If Bill needs any help. Send me!"

Soon Tigerlily chants a spell,
"Send Rupert on his way as well..."

"Wait, Rupert! Take my wand with you
So you can use its magic too."

"You'll have to ask your father for help!" Rupert tells Tigerlily. "That would be best," she nods. "But he's gone to Nutchester for the day and won't be back until tea-time!" "We can't wait till then!" gasps Rupert. "What if Bill's in trouble?" "Oh, dear!" wails Tigerlily. "I wish I'd never sent him to Between Land..." "That's it!" cries Rupert. "If you sent Bill, you can send *me* as well! I'll cross the smokescreen and try to find him!" "But what if you get stuck there too?" blinks Tigerlily.

Although Tigerlily isn't very happy with Rupert's plan, she finally agrees to send him to Between Land too. "Even if I get stuck, I'll still be able to help Bill!" he says. "I know he'd do the same for me..." As the others look on, Tigerlily waves her wand and chants another rhyme. "Let Rupert find his friend and then, return to Nutwood - safe again." "Good luck!" she calls, suddenly throwing the wand to Rupert. "You'd better take this with you. It might come in useful..."

RUPERT ENTERS BETWEEN LAND

What Rupert sees next makes him stare -
Bright stars and shapes float everywhere...

"White rabbits!" he laughs. "Fancy that!
They've come from a magician's hat..."

"Hello!" a rabbit calls. "That's new!
You've brought a magic wand with you..."

The rabbit learns why Rupert's there,
Then vanishes - into thin air!

Stepping forward through the coloured smoke, Rupert finds himself completely enveloped in a thick fog - which slowly clears to reveal an extraordinary landscape of bright colours and swirling stars... "Amazing!" he blinks. "I can see hearts and spades too, just like the ones on playing cards." As he looks around, Rupert soon realises that he is not alone. "Rabbits!" he smiles. "They're everywhere! I suppose they must be the ones that conjurers pull from their hats..."

"Hello!" says one of the rabbits, hopping up to Rupert. "Is that a wand you've got with you? We don't get many conjurers here! They normally stay on the other side, along with the audience..." "Oh, I'm not a conjurer!" says Rupert. "I've come to look for a friend of mine. I wonder if you've seen him?" "Perhaps," says the rabbit. "People come and go all day in Between Land!" Rupert is about to describe Bill, when the rabbit suddenly vanishes. "Magic!" he blinks. "It must have been called back..."

"I heard you ask about your chum,
I think I might have seen him come..."

"I can't see where Bill's gone at all!
Perhaps he'll hear me if I call?"

Three startled doves hear Rupert cry
And flutter up into the sky...

A glass of water starts to pour -
But more surprises lie in store!

Another rabbit sees what has happened and hops over to join Rupert... "Takes a bit of getting used to, doesn't it?" he laughs. "Did I hear you say you were looking for a friend?" "Yes," says Rupert. "A badger, called Bill. He's about the same size as me, with a blue jacket." "Stripy trousers!" smiles the rabbit. "I saw him arrive. He looked very startled at first, then went off to have a look round..." "Perhaps he'll hear me if I call his name?" thinks Rupert. "I hope he hasn't gone far!"

As Rupert calls Bill's name, he startles a group of white doves. They flutter up from their perch in a sudden flurry, disturbing a giant tumbler full of water that hovers mysteriously overhead. "Help!" gasps Rupert, peering up. "I'm going to get drenched." To his amazement, the water in the glass turns to a shower of brightly-coloured confetti. "That must be part of the act!" he blinks. "Nothing is what it seems around here! Between Land is so full of magic, *anything* could happen..."

RUPERT SUDDENLY DISAPPEARS

The ground begins to move below
His feet. "A playing card! Oh, no!"

Bright lights and stars shine all around
And Rupert tumbles to the ground...

"Poor thing! That looked a nasty knock!
It must have given you a shock..."

"Thank you," says Rupert. "I'm all right!"
But then he vanishes from sight...

Still marvelling at the sudden shower of confetti, Rupert suddenly feels the ground start to move beneath his feet - as if he's wearing roller-skates... "I'm standing on a huge playing card!" he gasps. "It's taking off like a flying carpet!" Rupert topples backwards as the card rears up. Lying on the ground, he sees it hover in the air then vanish with a dazzling flash of light. "Goodness!" he blinks. "I suppose a conjurer must have suddenly produced it as part of his act...."

As Rupert picks himself up, two rabbits hop forward. "That was a nasty fall!" says the first. "Thanks!" says Rupert. "But I wasn't hurt. It was just a surprise." "No harm done, then!" smiles the second rabbit. "Leaving Between Land is always a shock. You never get any warning, that's the problem. Here one moment, gone the next..." As the rabbit speaks, Rupert hears his voice growing fainter and fainter. The air suddenly fills with brightly coloured stars....

RUPERT FINDS BILL AT LAST

"It's all gone dark! Where am I now?
I'm being lifted up somehow!"

"A Conjurer!" blinks Rupert. "He
Looks just as mystified as me..."

"He must have called me with a spell...
Of course! And Bill is here as well!"

*"A **bear!**" the puzzled showman cries -*
He clearly can't believe his eyes.

From the colourful surroundings of Between Land, Rupert suddenly finds himself standing at the bottom of a tall, dark shaft. "What's happened?" he blinks. "Perhaps I've fallen down a rabbit hole?" Just then, he feels something tugging at his jersey. "Who's there?" he calls. Nobody answers, but the tugging gets stronger and stronger, until Rupert is lifted completely off his feet. To his astonishment, he emerges into a pool of dazzling light, where a giant conjurer stands...

As he looks round, Rupert sees that the Conjurer is obviously in the middle of a show. "He's pulled me out of a top hat!" he gasps. "Of course!" he must have been after one of the white rabbits..." The next moment, Rupert gets another shock as he spots Bill Badger, standing on the Magician's table. "Rupert!" calls his chum. "Whatever are you doing here?" "I don't know!" admits Rupert. "Neither do I!" groans the Conjurer. "Nothing like this has ever happened before..."

RUPERT PREPARES TO LEAVE

"Just listen!" the Magician beams.
"The crowd enjoyed your act, it seems..."

"This spectacle was specially planned -
Please give these two an extra hand!"

"Get ready, Bill! I'll tell you when...
To jump into the hat again!"

"Now!" Rupert calls. "It's time to go
We can't stay in a magic show..."

The chums are about to tell the Conjurer where they have come from when he remembers the audience and turns to acknowledge their applause. "They think you're part of the act!" he hisses. "Ladies and Gentlemen! A special hand please for my little assistants..." "Bravo!" calls a lady in the front row. "I don't know how he does it, but you have to admit they're a very lifelike pair of puppets!" "Puppets!" blinks Bill. "What a cheek! They'll expect us to start singing next!"

"Get ready to jump into the hat when I give the word," whispers Rupert as the chums take a bow. "All right," says Bill. "But I hope you know what you're doing..." "Now!" calls Rupert, waving Tigerlily's wand. "A spell to send us on our way - It's time we left without delay!" Bill clambers on to the brim of the hat while the Conjurer stares at the pair in astonishment. "Don't go yet!" he pleads. "You're a sensation..." "Sorry!" calls Rupert. "I can't explain. There's no time to lose!"

RUPERT MAKES A SPELL

The chums see the Magician's face
Then tumble backwards, down through space...

Stars swirl and dazzling colours flash -
They land together, with a crash!

"Come on, I'll use the wand to send
Us home now!" Rupert tells his friend.

Just as the two pals are all set,
Bill hears a cry, "Stop! Don't go yet..."

"Jump!" calls Rupert. He follows Bill into the hat, which opens below them like a long, deep tunnel... Looking up, he catches a last glimpse of the Conjurer peering balefully after the disappearing pals. For a few moments, they tumble down through darkness then suddenly find themselves dazzled by the bright colours and swirling stars of Between Land. "Look out!" cries Rupert as he falls on to Bill. "Thanks!" groans his chum. "Bit of a bumpy landing but I'm glad your spell worked!"

"Come on, Bill!" says Rupert, helping his chum to his feet. "We're half-way home now! Tigerlily was so worried about you that she lent me her magic wand..." "You mean you're going to make another spell?" asks Bill. "Of course!" smiles Rupert. "It's easy when you get the hang of it. All I need is a rhyme to send us back. I suppose it ought to mention Nutwood, to make sure we don't go to the wrong place." He is just about to wave the wand when Bill hears a sudden cry. "Wait a moment," he blinks.

RUPERT MEETS A LITTLE PRINCESS

The pals are both amazed to see
A girl who calls out, "Wait for me!"

"I'm lost!" she cries. "Do you two know
The way home? Which way should I go?"

"A magician has sent me here -
He tried to make me disappear..."

"I know I've been gone far too long -
I'm stranded here! The trick's gone wrong!"

As the chums look round, they see a distant figure running towards them... "It's a little girl!" says Bill, "She's calling for us to wait." "Thank goodness!" cries the girl as she nears the pals. "I thought I was stuck here, all alone. Please don't vanish, like all the rabbits." "Don't worry," says Rupert. "We were about to go back to Nutwood, but you've caught us, just in time..." "Whatever's the matter?" asks Bill. "Why have you been crying? Is there anything we can do to help?"

The little girl is so upset that she starts crying again as she tells Rupert and Bill her story... "It's my birthday today!" she sniffs. "A wizard came to my party and did a trick to make me disappear... He said I'd only be gone for a few minutes, but that was ages ago! I think the trick must have gone wrong, and now I'll have to stay here forever and ever!" "Oh, dear!" says Rupert. "It's lucky you found us. We can send you home with our wand, I expect. It's certainly worth a try..."

RUPERT HELPS THE PRINCESS

*The chums prepare to make a spell -
"We'll take you home and come as well!"*

*Stars flash and suddenly they all
Appear in a great palace hall...*

*"Papa! I'm back. The spell went wrong,
Then more magicians came along..."*

*"More conjurers? Arrest the lot!
I've had enough of all their rot!"*

The two chums hold hands with the little girl, while Rupert thinks of a spell... "Where do you live?" he asks. "In the Palace, with my parents," she says. "We were together with the wizard, in the Great Hall..." "Reverse the magic, take us all, back to the Palace's Great Hall." There is a flash of stars and the pals find themselves standing in a splendid hall, where a King is angrily cursing a wretched-looking magician. "Knave!" he bellows. "Where is my beloved daughter?"

"Papa!" the little girl cries. "Here I am! There's no need to worry. Everything's all right! I met two magicians who brought me home..." "Poppet!" beams the King. "Thank goodness you're safe!" "Sire!" stammers the Wizard. "I sincerely regret... most unfortunate... all a mistake." "Enough!" barks the King. "The Princess is safe, but no thanks to you! Magicians are a menace! Guards! Arrest them all! Take these sorcerers to the dungeons. I'll decide what to do with them later...."

RUPERT IS SENT TO THE DUNGEONS

The Wizard quails as they all go
Down to the dungeons, deep below...

"In there!" a guard scowls angrily.
"I'd lock you up and lose the key!"

"My spell's to blame! It went wrong when
I called the Princess back again..."

"The main thing's that she's safe and sound -
It's lucky we were both around!"

"This way!" says one of the sentries sternly. "Follow me..." "Oh, dear!" sighs the Wizard as he clambers down a gloomy flight of stairs. "What a disaster! I've never known the King get so cross. He's normally kind-hearted, but I don't think he'll ever forgive me for making the Princess disappear." "Can't say I blame him!" snaps the guard as he slams the heavy door. "Frightening a little girl on her birthday! It's just as well for you that your friends here brought her back."

"I'm sorry!" sighs the Wizard. "This is all my fault. I should never have tried to make the Princess vanish! The spell's always worked with rabbits and glasses of water, but when she didn't come back I was so flustered I didn't know what to do..." "Don't worry!" says Rupert. "She's safe and sound now, although it's lucky that Bill and I were in Between Land." "Between Land!" blinks the magician. "So it really does exist! I've always wanted to see what it was like..."

RUPERT AND BILL ESCAPE

"Between Land is the place for you -
Get ready and we'll both come too..."

The dungeon fades - bright stars appear -
"Between Land!" Rupert smiles. "We're here!"

"What fun! These objects must have been
Sent here to stop them being seen..."

"Don't go yet!" the magician cries.
But both pals fade before his eyes...

Rupert smiles. "Between Land is just the place for you to stay until the King calms down. It's better than being locked up in the dungeons!" Waving Tigerlily's wand he starts to chant a rhyme. "Please take us from this gloomy cell by granting me another spell. The Land Between is where we need - please take us there now, with all speed!" Swirling stars fill the air and the cell's darkness gives way to bright colours and dazzling light. "Between Land!" blinks the Wizard.

As the Wizard takes his bearings, he gazes in wonder at the procession of strange objects floating through the air... "Of course!" he laughs. "Other magicians are doing vanishing tricks all the time. Cards, eggs, handkerchiefs... what fun! If I stay here long enough, I might even get some new ideas for my act." Turning to the pals, he blinks in amazement as they suddenly vanish in a flash of light. "Bless me!" he gasps. "What a surprise! I didn't even see him wave his wand..."

RUPERT RETURNS TO NUTWOOD

*The two chums fall through space and then
Emerge in Nutwood once again!*

*"I'm glad you're back - you had good luck.
If things went wrong, you'd still be stuck!"*

*The Conjurer recites a spell -
"Good! Now the cones have gone as well…"*

*"We'll put the rest of these away -
Enough of fireworks for one day!"*

To their astonishment, Rupert and Bill find themselves suddenly snatched out of Between Land and back into Nutwood… "Hurrah!" cheer their chums as they tumble through the smokescreen and land at the feet of Tigerlily's father. "Good!" he laughs. "My spell has worked! I summoned you home as soon as I heard what had happened. It is very unwise to meddle with magic. Good fortune smiled on you this time, but if things had gone differently you could have been stuck between worlds!"

Turning from the startled chums, the Conjurer waves his hands over the smouldering cones and chants another spell. "This screen of smoke must disappear, it is no longer needed here!" To everyone's amazement, the fireworks fade away in a shimmer of stars, leaving nothing but a wisp of smoke. "Come!" the Conjurer tells Tigerlily. "We must store the remainder safely." "So much for fireworks!" smiles Rupert. "They were fun but from now on I think I'll stick to sparklers!"

Mrs. Trunk's Strawberry Flan

A simple pudding for the strawberry season....

INGREDIENTS
50g (2oz) caster sugar
50g (2oz) plain flour
2 eggs
350g (12oz) fresh strawberries
3 tablespoons apricot (or strawberry) jam
2 tablespoons water
A small pat of butter
2 teaspoons caster sugar
1 teaspoon plain flour

1. Pre-heat oven to 180 C (350 F), Gas Mark 4.

2. Grease a 23cm (9") round cake (sandwich) tin with a small pat of butter. Sprinkle with 2 teaspoons of caster sugar and shake to coat evenly. Add 1 teaspoon of plain flour and shake again. Tip out any excess.

3. Crack two eggs into a deep mixing bowl. Add 50g (2oz) caster sugar and whisk vigorously (or beat with an electric mixer) until the mixture is thick and creamy.

4. Sieve 50g (2oz) flour on to the surface of the mixture and fold in gently with a metal spoon.

5. Pour mixture into the prepared cake tin.

6. Bake in the oven (middle shelf) at 180 C (350F), Gas Mark 4 for 20-25 minutes, until the risen sponge shrinks from the side of the tin and springs back when lightly pressed.

7. Turn out on to a wire rack and leave to cool.

8. Hull and wash the strawberries. Pat them dry and cut in half.

9. Place the sponge base on a serving plate and cover with strawberries.

10. Put 3 tablespoons of jam into a small saucepan and add 2 tablespoons of water. Stirring constantly, heat until boiling then simmer gently for one minute.

11. Sieve the melted jam into a bowl. Pour evenly over the strawberries. Allow to cool.

12. Serve flan in slices with cream or ice-cream as preferred.

(You will need to ask an adult to help you with this recipe)

These two pictures look identical, but there are ten differences between them. Can you spot them all? *Answers on page 109*

87

How carefully can you colour these two pictures?

Rupert's Crossword Puzzle

See if you can complete this crossword. Most of the answers can be found in stories from this year's annual . . .

ACROSS

4. Eaten by mites? (5,5)
5. Nutwood's farmer (5)
7. Nutwood family with thatched cottage (4)
11. Disappear (6)
13. Moke (6)
15. Reminds Rupert what to buy (4)
16. Nutwood's oldest inhabitant (6,5)
19. Single figure (3)
20. King's daughter (8)
21. Request (3)
22. Makes you laugh (4)
23. Bunny (6)
26. Scarecrow owned by 5 across (7)
27. Noisy Firework (6)
29. Bucket (4)
30. Direction finder (7)
32. Used by 12 down to deliver 20 down (6)
35. Foolish month (5)
37. Nutwood's policeman (7)
38. Cut in summer, dried and stored (3)
39. Rupert's largest chum (6)
41. Mislaid (4)
43. Last month of the year (8)

DOWN

1. Detain (6)
2. Burn slowly (8)
3. Fire extinguisher (5)
6. Desire- granted magically (4)
8. Mechanical device (7)
9. Christmas decoration (6)
10. Imps' leader (4)
12. Father Christmas (5)
13. Prison cell- underground (7)
14. Maker of magic (8)
17. Freddy and Ferdy's surname (3)
18. Funny man (6)
20. Gifts (8)
24. Daughter of The Chinese Conjurer (9)
25. Noisy collision (5)
27. Rupert's best friend (4)
28. November blaze (7)
31. Sweetener (5)
33. Nutwood guineapig (7)
34. Nutwood mouse (6)
35. A pug. Rupert's friend. (4)
36. Lapland creature. Tows 32 across for 12 down (8)
38. Stop (4)
40. Top card (3)
42. Pair (3)

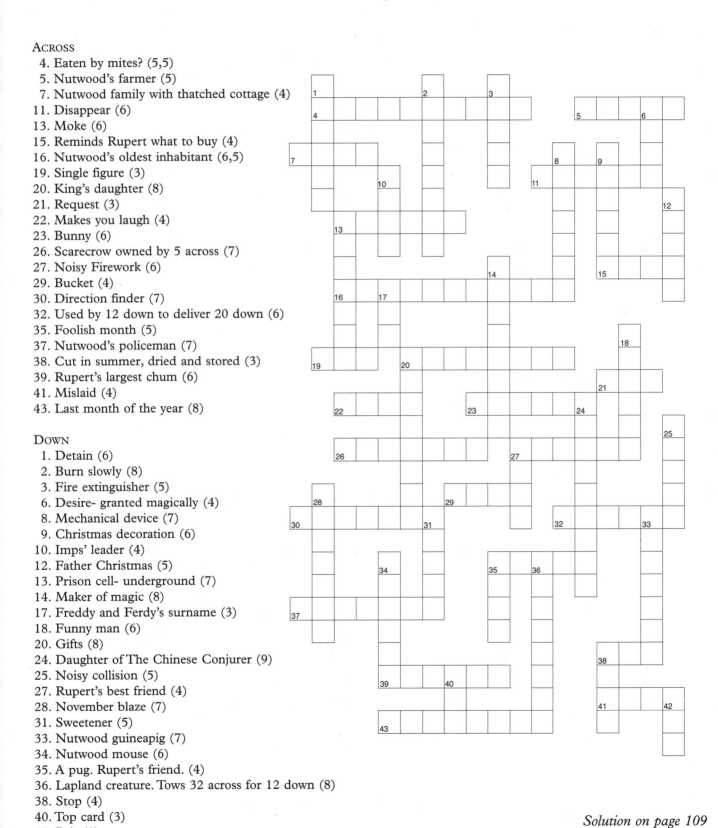

Solution on page 109

RUPERT and

*It's nearly Christmas time once more –
And Rupert's at the village store…*

Winter has arrived in Nutwood. Bonfire Night is over and everyone's thoughts have begun to turn to Christmas… "A Christmas cake!" smiles Mr. Chimp as Rupert hands him Mrs. Bear's list. "I can tell that's what you're making! Mrs. Badger was in earlier, buying all the things for hers. Candied peel! That's what you need. And lots of currants and raisins. Tell your mother I've put some glace cherries at the bottom of the basket…"

the Christmas Cake

*"I think that's all that's on your list -
I hope there's nothing we have missed!"*

*"Well done!" says Mrs. Bear. "Now you
Can help me make the cake mix too..."*

Rupert hurries home with the basket of shopping. "Well done!" smiles Mrs. Bear. "We'll make a start straightaway. You can help me measure everything out..." Rupert's mother reads through the recipe carefully. "There are so many things to remember!" she laughs. "Eggs, butter, flour..." "Raisins!" adds Rupert. "I've measured those already." "Good!" says Mrs. Bear. "Tip them in with everything else. Now we need to give it all a good stir..."

*"Flour, eggs and butter, fruit and spice,
Now raisins, Rupert. Those look nice..."*

RUPERT GETS A CHRISTMAS WISH

*"Come on now, Rupert! Time to make
A Christmas wish and stir the cake..."*

*"What do I really want? More snow?
Or extra presents? I don't know!"*

*"The decorations! Try to see
If you can find their tin for me."*

*"Hurrah!" cheers Rupert. "They're in here,
The same tin we use every year..."*

When the cake ingredients have been mixed together, Rupert's mother hands him the spoon to give them all a stir. "Don't forget to make a wish!" she says as Rupert climbs up to reach the bowl. "Keep it secret and it might come true!" Rupert stirs the cake excitedly. "What shall I wish for?" he thinks. "I've already written my list to Santa. Perhaps I ought to ask for snow? I can't decide!" Rupert declares at last. "I'll save my wish for later, till there's something I *really* want..."

"Well done!" says Mrs. Bear. "The next thing you can do is look out the cake decorations..." "Hurrah!" cheers Rupert. "The little snowman and Santa Claus. They're in an old tin aren't they?" "That's right," nods his mother. "Try looking at the back of the cupboard. I think that's where I put it." Rupert rummages through the jars and packets until he comes to what he's after. "This is it!" he smiles. "They've been here all year, just waiting for Christmas to come round again..."

RUPERT FINDS THE DECORATIONS

"The Snowman, Santa and his sack,
I'm always glad to see them back!"

"The reindeer with a little sleigh -
And there's their tree, for Christmas Day..."

"We'll pop this in the oven, then
I'll ice it when it's cool again..."

That evening, Rupert asks if he
Can keep the figures after tea...

While Mrs. Bear pours all the cake mixture into the baking tin, Rupert takes out the decorations and sets them on the table... "Hello!" he smiles. "I'm glad to see you all again. It really feels as though Christmas is on its way when you appear!" "They are rather special, aren't they?" laughs Rupert's mother. "We've had them for years!" "If I was a decoration, I'd look forward to being put on a cake," says Rupert. "All that white icing must be just like real snow..."

At last, Mrs. Bear is ready to put the cake into the oven. "It will take hours to bake!" she says. "And almost as long to cool down..." "Can we do the icing today?" asks Rupert. "No!" laughs his mother. "You need to keep Christmas cakes for a while before you ice them. We'll wait another day for that." Later that evening, as Rupert is getting ready for bed, he asks his parents if he can take the Christmas figures up to his room. "Of course!" smiles Mrs. Bear. "Keep them safe until we're ready..."

He takes the figures carefully
And sets them out where he can see...

"Goodnight!" he smiles. "I'll see you when
It's morning and I wake again!"

Much later, Rupert wakes to hear
The sound of sleighbells somewhere near...

He gasps, astonished at the sight
That greets him - Santa's sleigh in flight!

Carrying the tin of Christmas cake decorations upstairs, Rupert clears off his bedside table then carefully arranges all the little figures... "It looks just like an enormous cake!" he smiles. "I expect they'll be much happier up here than staying shut in a tin!" As he climbs into bed and settles down to sleep, Santa and the others appear even more lifelike, casting long shadows from the lamp. "You can stay here until the cake has been iced," Rupert murmurs drowsily.

Later that night, Rupert wakes from a dream about Santa Claus and his flying sleigh... "It was so real, I was sure I could hear the harness bells of the reindeer!" he blinks. "I *can* hear bells!" he gasps, sitting up suddenly. To his astonishment, the cake decorations have vanished from the table and a tiny sleigh is flying round and round the room, with Santa at the reins and the Snowman hanging on behind. "I don't believe it!" he laughs delightedly. "They're real! They've come to life!"

RUPERT SEES A TINY SLEIGH

"Hello!" the Snowman calls. "We thought
We'd slip out without being caught..."

"A special journey! Time to go!
We'll be back in the morning though..."

"Wait!" Rupert calls. "I'll let you out
And make sure nobody's about..."

He throws the window open wide
And peers into the dark outside...

Hardly daring to move, Rupert leans forward for a better view of the sleigh... "Hello!" calls the Snowman. "Sorry to wake you up! We were hoping to leave without disturbing you." "Leave?" gasps Rupert. "That's right," nods the little Santa. "A special journey! No time to explain everything now, but if all goes according to plan we should be back in plenty of time to go on your Christmas cake." "Where are you going?" blinks Rupert. "Out of the window!" laughs Santa. "Then up and away!"

Pulling on his dressing gown, Rupert draws the curtains wide and climbs up to open the window. He peers out at the darkness, then back to the tiny flying sleigh. "Thanks, Rupert!" calls the Snowman. "Nobody out there, I hope. It wouldn't do for anyone else to see us flying about like this!". "No," says Rupert. "Everyone else in Nutwood is sound asleep..." "Splendid!" cries Santa. "Then we're all set! If you leave the window ajar, we'll try to be back before it gets light."

RUPERT'S WISH COMES TRUE

"I wish that I was tiny too -
Then I could come along with you!"

Stars swirl all round and Rupert shrinks -
"The Christmas wish I saved!" he thinks.

The sleigh turns back again and lands
On the low chest where Rupert stands...

The decorations heard him call -
"You're welcome to come, now you're small.

"I wish I could come with you!" says Rupert as he stands aside to let the little sleigh pass. All at once, the air fills with swirling stars and he suddenly feels himself falling slowly down and down. "I...I'm shrinking!" he gasps. "It must be the wish left over from when I made the christmas cake. I didn't use it earlier, so perhaps it will come true now? I wonder where the Snowman and Santa can be going? I do hope they'll let me join them. I'm sure I'm the right size to fit on their sleigh..."

To Rupert's delight, the little sleigh turns back, then swoops down to land on the chest where he is standing. "I didn't know you could change size!" calls the Snowman. "It makes quite a difference! You're welcome to come along with us if you want to..." "Hop up here!" smiles Santa. "Bit of a tight fit, I'm afraid, but I'm sure we can manage." "Thank you!" says Rupert. "I didn't know that I could change size either, but now I have, I can't wait to find out what you're up to."

RUPERT HAS A SLEIGH RIDE

The sleigh sets off without delay -
"Hold tight Rupert, we're on our way!"

The travellers think no-one sees
Their sleigh soar high above the trees...

The Wise Old Owl blinks with surprise
As Santa's sleigh takes to the skies...

It soon leaves Nutwood far below
But still has many miles to go...

As soon as everyone is safely aboard, the tiny reindeer pulls the sleigh forward then springs up into the air... "It's just like the real Santa's sleigh!" thinks Rupert. "I wonder if they're on their way to deliver a sack of presents?" Soaring out of the window, the sleigh glides over Rupert's garden and up past the rooftops of Nutwood. "Everybody's asleep!" laughs Rupert. "There's Bill's house and that's Podgy's down there! They'd all be amazed if they could see me..."

Unknown to Rupert, not everyone in Nutwood is asleep as the little sleigh sets off... "Bless me!" blinks the Wise Old Owl. "Christmas Eve already? I thought it was weeks away! That sleigh looks a bit overloaded. Santa must have taken on a few more helpers..." Leaving Nutwood far behind, the reindeer climbs higher and higher, until the sleigh is up among the clouds in a dark, star-filled sky. "Outdoors!" cheers the Snowman happily. "It's been years since I've seen a sight like this..."

RUPERT VISITS SANTA'S CASTLE

*"We're on our way to somewhere you
Have often sent your letters to..."*

*"It's Santa's Castle!" Rupert blinks
"But what do they want there?" he thinks...*

*"We're going to the workshops where
We were first made!" explain the pair...*

*"An open window! That's the way..."
They fly in on the little sleigh.*

As the little sleigh flies on through the night, Rupert asks his companions where they are going... "Back to where we came from!" says Santa. "Before we were sent to Mr. Chimp's shop in Nutwood!" "Where we were made!" explains the Snowman. "Santa Claus' castle!" gasps Rupert as he spots a distant building. "I should have guessed that was where we were going. Do all decorations come from there?" "Proper ones do!" nods the Snowman. "From the same workshops as puppets and dolls."

Although Rupert has visited Santa's castle before, he has never been to the workshops where toys are made... "Next to the stores," says the Snowman. "Busiest place in the whole castle, during the day. I don't think there'll be anyone there now..." The little sleigh circles over the courtyard, then swoops down towards the window of a tall tower. "Hurrah!" laughs the Snowman. "Just like old times!" Rupert is amazed at all the toys. "Puppets! Dolls! There's even a Noah's Ark!" he laughs.

RUPERT LANDS IN THE WORKSHOPS

Inside the workshop toys surround
The sleigh as it flies all around...

"Oh, dear!" sighs Santa. "These are all
Too big for us. We're only small!"

"Down there!" calls Rupert. "That looks more
The sort of thing you're looking for..."

"Well done!" says Santa. "Now let's see
Where what we've come to get can be..."

Flying into the cluttered workshop, the little sleigh passes over benches piled high with half-finished toys still waiting for a final coat of paint. "We're nearly there!" says the Snowman excitedly. "Nearly!" nods Santa. "But I can't see the right shelves yet. All these are far too big..." "Too big?" asks Rupert. "For us!" says the little man. "We've come to look for decorations, you see. Toys and games are all very well, but there's another bench where everything small is made..."

"Over there!" calls Rupert as he peers around the workshop. Standing on a bench are Christmas decorations of all kinds, from snowmen and robins to Christmas trees and fairies. "Well done!" says Santa. "This is the place we were after. All we have to do now is find what we're looking for..." "Can I help?" asks Rupert. "Perhaps," says Santa. "We might need you to scramble up and open one of those drawers." "I wonder what they want?" thinks Rupert. "More toys to deliver, I suppose..."

RUPERT IS DISCOVERED

The visitors search everywhere
But what they want just isn't there...

Then, suddenly, they get a fright,
Caught in a dazzling beam of light!

Two guards appear. "What's this?" they shout.
"We can't have toys marching about!"

"They're not toys!" Rupert says. "You see,
They've come from Nutwood, just like me!"

While Rupert looks on, the little figures busily search the whole bench, peering into every jar and container they can reach. "They must be here somewhere!" says the Snowman. "Perhaps in this big chest of drawers?" As he speaks the three companions are suddenly caught in the glare of a dazzling light. "Who's there?" calls a voice. "They're only toys!" says a second. "You're right!" says the first. "But I'm sure I saw them moving about. Look at that little snowman!"

Squinting into the light, Rupert sees two of Santa's castle guards. "Very odd, this!" says the first. "We can't have toys running about on their own!" "We're not toys!" says the little Father Christmas. "We're decorations..." "From Nutwood!" adds Rupert. "We flew here in a sleigh." "Visitors, eh?" says the second soldier. "That's different! Guests are allowed to visit the castle, but they've got to get permission from the Chief Clerk. We'd better go and see him straightaway!"

RUPERT TALKS TO THE CLERK

*The visitors are taken to
The Chief Clerk. "He'll know what to do!"*

*He looks up as a sentry knocks -
"Come in, you two! What's in that box?"*

*"They're little visitors we found,
In the Workshop, looking around!"*

*"Please," Santa says, "We came to see
If we could decorate our tree..."*

Lifted into a little box, Rupert and the decorations find themselves being transported across the castle courtyard, to the Chief Clerk's office. "Oh, dear!" sighs Rupert. "It must be his busiest time of year. I hope he won't be too cross at being disturbed. The guards climb a flight of steps to a cluttered room where the Clerk is still hard at work, writing lists of presents in a heavy ledger... "Come in!" he calls. "Not often I get a call from the Night Watch! Is anything wrong?"

Santa's Clerk peers at the box the guards are carrying. "Toys!" he shrugs. "A snowman, Father Christmas and a little bear." "Yes, sir!" explains a soldier. "We found them in the Workshops, wandering about on their own..." "Goodness!" blinks the Clerk. "What were they up to?" "Looking for something, if you ask me!" says the other sentry. "That's right!" nods the little Santa. "We didn't mean any harm. All we want are some Christmas decorations, for the tree on our cake..."

RUPERT IS TAKEN TO SANTA

The Clerk blinks at the strange request –
"Tree decorations! I'll be blessed!"

"I've never heard the like before –
We'll check with Santa to make sure..."

The Clerk climbs to the topmost floor,
Then knocks on Santa's bedroom door...

"I'm sorry, sir! Some guests to see –
They've called quite unexpectedly!"

"Decorations for your tree?" gasps the Clerk. "Yes," says the Snowman. "To go on a cake!" the Clerk blinks. "It's highly irregular, you know! I don't think we've ever had a request like this before..." "*Please?*" asks Rupert. "It would look nice!" "Baubles," murmurs the Clerk. "Tinsel, I suppose you want a star to go on top as well..." "If it's not too much trouble," smiles the Snowman. "We'll see," says the Clerk. "I'll have to ask Santa what he thinks..."

After climbing to the top of the tower, the castle guards hesitate nervously as the Clerk knocks at the door to Santa's room. "Yes?" comes a voice from within, "Who's there?" "Sorry to disturb you, sir!" says the Clerk. "I'm afraid we've got some unexpected visitors." "At this time of night?" blinks Santa. "Goodness me! I suppose you'd better show them in." "They are in!" says the Clerk. "I've taken the liberty of bringing them with me." "Where?" says Santa. "I can't see any guests..."

*"Guests?" Santa blinks. "Yes, sir. They flew
Here in a sleigh, to visit you..."*

*The Clerk explains - "They're from a cake -
And have a strange request to make!"*

*As Santa looks more closely, he
Blinks in amazement, "Goodness me!"*

*"It's Rupert Bear! Can this be true?
What is it that you'd like to do?"*

"These are the visitors!" explains the Clerk. "They were found wandering round the warehouse, looking for Christmas tree decorations..." "But those are decorations!" blinks Santa. "Cake decorations," nods the Clerk. "They flew in through the window on a tiny sleigh." "How strange!" says Santa. "We make decorations for cakes, don't we?" "Yes!" nods the Clerk. "But these are the first to come back as visitors. They say they want to decorate the tree on their cake..."

As Santa Claus peers more closely at the tiny figures he suddenly blinks in astonishment... "Bless me!" he gasps. "I recognise one of these chaps. You're not a decoration! You're Rupert Bear, from Nutwood!" "That's right, sir," says Rupert. "I shrank to this size to come on a special journey. These are my mother's cake decorations. I'm sure they didn't mean to cause all this fuss. It's just that they'd like to put some decorations on their christmas tree, like everyone else."

RUPERT PERSUADES SANTA

*"I see!" he laughs. "Can't see why not!
Let's go and look at what we've got..."*

*"Tree decorations, let me see...
Down to the Workshops - follow me!"*

*"This looks the right place!" Santa cries.
"Decorations of every size..."*

*He opens up a tiny drawer.
"In here, I think. I'll just make sure..."*

To Rupert's relief, Santa breaks into a broad grin. "It's a very unusual request!" he chuckles. "But I don't see why not. Decorating the tree is part of the Christmas fun, after all! No reason to miss out, just because you're tiny..." Pulling on his dressing gown, he takes the box from his Clerk and tells the delighted decorations to climb back in. "Off we go, then!" he calls. "I'm sure we'll be able to find all the things you need. Come along, everyone, follow me."

"Decorations..." murmurs Santa as he leads the way down to the workshops. "I'm sure they're here, somewhere! Let me see..." Peering over the edge of the box, Rupert spots the bench where the Snowman and his companion have left their sleigh, with the little reindeer waiting patiently. "Here we are!" chuckles Santa. "Tree decorations, cake decorations, all sorts of decorations..." Opening one of the little drawers, he peers inside as Rupert and the others look on expectantly.

RUPERT RECEIVES A GIFT

"Here!" Santa smiles. "This sack's for when
You get back to Nutwood again..."

"Well done!" the others cheer. "Now we
Must leave for home immediately!"

The figures climb into their sleigh -
Which takes to the air straightaway...

"Goodbye!" calls Santa Claus, "Have fun!
A Merry Christmas, everyone!"

"Got it!" beams Santa. "These are what we need..." Reaching into the drawer, he lifts out a little sack, just like the one on the tiny sleigh. "For you!" he smiles, handing the bag to Rupert. "Open it when you get back to Nutwood." The little figures gather round excitedly. "Well done!" cheers the Snowman. "I should have known that Santa wouldn't let us down!" "Success!" beams the tiny Father Christmas. "I suppose we'd better be leaving soon. We ought to get back before morning."

When Rupert and the decorations are safely aboard, the little sleigh takes off with a jingle of bells... "Safe journey!" beams Santa. "I'll be loading up my own sleigh soon!" "Happy Christmas!" nods the Clerk. "Highly irregular proceedings but I'm glad we were able to help." "Goodbye!" calls the Snowman, waving his hat. "Nice to see the old workshop looking so lively..." Rupert waves back to Santa as the sleigh flies over the courtyard and up into the star-spangled sky.

RUPERT'S FRIENDS ARE DELIGHTED

"Thanks, Rupert!" says the Snowman. "You
Must help us dress the tree now too..."

"Let's look inside the sack! I say!
They'll make a wonderful display..."

The little sleigh speeds through the night
To Nutwood. "They're still sleeping tight!"

It flies to Rupert's house and then
Flits in at the window again...

"Thanks, Rupert!" says the Snowman. "I'm glad you came with us." "So am I!" smiles Rupert. "I knew Santa would understand. He's always so kind and jolly!" "Let's have a look in the sack!" says the little Father Christmas. "I can't wait to see what he's given us." "Just a peek!" laughs Rupert. Opening the bag carefully, Rupert reaches inside and pulls out a gleaming silver ball. "Perfect!" says Santa. "There's tinsel too!" calls the Snowman. "I can't wait to put everything on our tree..."

It is still dark as the sleigh reaches Nutwood, with everyone still slumbering peacefully... "If only they knew!" smiles Rupert. The next moment, the reindeer swoops down towards Rupert's house, flitting in at the open window. "Phew!" gasps the Snowman. "We made it!" "What a journey!" chuckles the little Santa. "Well done, Prancer! The old man's team won't be any swifter than you..." The little reindeer shakes his harness with pleasure and swoops down towards Rupert's bedside table...

RUPERT DECORATES THE TREE

The little sleigh swoops down and lands
Just next to where the bare tree stands...

"Let's set to work!" the Snowman cries.
"This tinsel is the perfect size!"

At last they're finished. "That looks great,
Well done!" yawns Rupert. "Gosh! It's late..."

"Goodnight!" he calls. "I'd better go
Back to my bed now, down below..."

The little tree is still standing, all alone, on Rupert's bedside table... "Let's decorate it straightaway!" calls the Snowman. "I can't wait to begin!" "Good idea!" laughs Santa. "Here's some tinsel you can make a start with." "It's just like a real tree!" says Rupert. "These decorations are the perfect size." "There are lots here!" says Santa. "I'll help you with some of the baubles." "Just wait!" beams the Snowman. "This will be one of the best-dressed trees in Nutwood..."

In no time at all, the Christmas tree is completely covered in decorations. The last one is a silver star, which Rupert reaches up and fixes on top. "Lovely!" he yawns. "Time you were off to bed!" smiles the little Santa. "It's been a long night." "I *am* rather sleepy!" says Rupert. "Thanks for letting me come with you." "Thank you for helping!" says the Snowman. Rupert jumps down from the table to his bed, which seems like a giant trampoline. "Happy Christmas!" calls the little Santa...

The bed's so soft that Rupert sighs
And falls fast asleep, where he lies.

Next morning, Mrs. Bear's amazed
To find that Rupert's still half-dazed...

"I had a dream, about the tree,"
Says Rupert, yawning sleepily...

"It does seem to have changed somehow -
*Yes, look! It's **decorated** now!"*

Rupert's bed feels so soft and comfortable that he falls asleep almost straightaway... The sleigh ride, Santa's castle and scenes from the cluttered workshop fill his dreams until Mrs. Bear comes to wake him next morning. "Hello!" she smiles. "Why are you wearing your dressing gown? Don't say you fell asleep before you got into bed?" "I suppose I must have done!" blinks Rupert. "I had a wonderful dream about Christmas!" "I'm not surprised!" laughs his mother. "It must be the cake decorations..."

"The decorations!" cries Rupert. "That's what my dream was about. I shrank until I was the same size as them, then we all went to Santa's castle to get some tinsel and baubles for their tree..." "The tree!" gasps Mrs. Bear. "It does look different from how I remembered it..." "Isn't it lovely!" says Rupert. "Covered in tinsel, just like ours! I can't wait to see it on top of the cake." "Neither can I," smiles his mother happily. "Neither can I!"

108

Follow Rupert every day

in The Daily Express

John Harrold.

ANSWERS TO PUZZLES:

(P.87) SPOT THE DIFFERENCE

1) House missing from village; 2) Cloud missing from sky; 3) Branch missing from tree; 4) Button missing from Bill's waistcoat; 5) Turn-ups missing from Algy's trousers; 6) Car: rear window missing; 7) Car: door handle missing; 8) Car: door-hinges missing; 9) Car: steering-wheel missing; 10) Car: lamp missing.

(P.89) RUPERT'S CROSSWORD

Across:
4. Rusty Metal, 5. Brown, 7. Bear, 11.Vanish, 13. Donkey, 15. List, 16. Gaffer Jarge, 19. One, 20. Princess, 21. Ask, 22. Joke, 23. Rabbit, 26. Odmedod, 27. Banger, 29. Pail, 30. Compass, 32. Sleigh, 35. April, 37. Growler, 38. Hay, 39. Edward, 41. Lost, 43. December.

Down:
1. Arrest, 2. Smoulder, 3. Water, 6. Wish, 8. Machine, 9. Tinsel, 10. King, 12. Santa, 13. Dungeon, 14. Magician, 17. Fox, 18. Jester, 20. Presents, 24. Tigerlily, 25. Crash, 27. Bill, 28. Bonfire, 31. Sugar, 33. Gregory, 34. Willie, 35. Algy, 36. Reindeer, 38. Halt, 40. Ace, 42. Two.

John Harrold.